PUFFIN BOOKS

Classroom Demons

ke Lancing lives in Somerset. When not writing
bout adventure-seeking, football-playing angels,
e spends his time avoiding work, listening to
ry uncool music, growing his hair and helping
e government to catch spies.* He jumped out
a plane once because it seemed like a good
ea at the time.

One of these things might not be *entirely*
rue.

Books by Jake Lancing

DEMON DEFENDERS:
CLASSROOM DEMONS

DEMON DEFENDERS:
ZOMBIES IN THE HOUSE

Classroom Demons

JAKE LANCING

PUFFIN

With special thanks to David J. Gatward

PUFFIN BOOKS

Published by the Penguin Group
Penguin Books Ltd, 80 Strand, London WC2R 0RL, England
Penguin Group (USA) Inc., 375 Hudson Street, New York, New York 10014, USA
Penguin Group (Canada), 90 Eglinton Avenue East, Suite 700,
Toronto, Ontario, Canada M4P 2Y3
(a division of Pearson Penguin Canada Inc.)
Penguin Ireland, 25 St Stephen's Green, Dublin 2, Ireland
(a division of Penguin Books Ltd)
Penguin Group (Australia), 250 Camberwell Road,
Camberwell, Victoria 3124, Australia
(a division of Pearson Australia Group Pty Ltd)
Penguin Books India Pvt Ltd, 11 Community Centre, Panchsheel Park,
New Delhi – 110 017, India
Penguin Group (NZ), 67 Apollo Drive, Rosedale, North Shore 0632, New Zealand
(a division of Pearson New Zealand Ltd)
Penguin Books (South Africa) (Pty) Ltd, 24 Sturdee Avenue,
Rosebank, Johannesburg 2196, South Africa

Penguin Books Ltd, Registered Offices: 80 Strand, London WC2R 0RL, England

puffinbooks.com

First published 2009
1

Text copyright © Hothouse Fiction Ltd, 2009
All rights reserved

Set in Bembo by Palimpsest Book Production Limited,
Grangemouth, Stirlingshire
Made and printed in England by Clays Ltd, St Ives plc

British Library Cataloguing in Publication Data
A CIP catalogue record for this book is available from the British Library

ISBN: 978–0–141–32458–6

www.greenpenguin.co.uk

For Su

Contents

I

Trouble in Paradise

'This is my most brilliant idea yet,' muttered Alex, his ice-blue eyes glinting mischievously under his blond fringe.

It was a beautiful day in Heaven. The kind of day when it seemed like nothing could possibly go wrong. Alex and his best friend and team-mate Big House were in a large garden, crouched behind an enormous ornamental pond, complete with dolphin-shaped fountain.

House eyed the sculpture nervously.

'What are we doing?' he whispered, trying to make sure his wings didn't knock into Alex and

1

send him sprawling into the water. Like the rest of his body, House's wings were several times larger than average and, as everyone at Cloud Nine Academy had learned to their cost, seemed to act as accident magnets.

'Well, it's not fair, is it?' said Alex. 'The Wingers are the new Cloud Nine five-a-side football champions, aren't we?'

'Yeah –'

'But there haven't exactly been any celebrations, have there?' continued Alex. 'Where are the screaming crowds, the banners, the waving flags? Everyone should know we've won, don't you think?'

'But it was just a school footie tournament,' said House. 'It's not like we're champions of the universe or anything.'

Alex turned away.

'Check this out,' he said, pulling a large red bottle from his pocket.

House read the label: *Warning – Will Stain Clothes!* He winced. This didn't look good.

'Do the rest of the team know about this?'

'They soon will,' said Alex. 'Here they come now.'

From behind a nearby hedge, three winged

figures darted towards them: a girl in a striking red baseball cap, a boy with scruffy black hair, and a much smaller boy wearing very large glasses.

'Hi,' said Alex. 'You all ready for this?'

'Ready for what?' asked the girl, who was wearing combats, heavy boots, a zebra-stripe top – and a quiver and bow on her back. 'What are you up to this time, Alex?'

'He's got a bottle of dye, Cherry,' sighed House.

'What're you going to do with it?' asked Cherry, turning to Alex.

'Whatever it is,' said the dark-haired boy, 'it's bound to be something stupid that gets us into trouble.'

'*Respite*, I'm hurt,' replied Alex, not looking it at all. 'When have I ever got you into trouble?'

'About as many times as I've told you not to call me "Respite". It makes me sound like a total wuss.'

'Sorry. Spit.'

'Better.'

The last member of the gang, Inchy, who barely came up to House's waist, looked through his thick spectacles at the bottle in Alex's hands.

'So what are you going to do with that, then?'

'*We*,' corrected Alex, 'are going to dye the fountain red.'

'Er, why?' asked Spit.

'Red's our team colour, isn't it? So everyone will know it was The Wingers who won the championship. It's like a celebration!'

'But everyone already knows we won,' replied Cherry.

'And because of that, it'll be really obvious that it was us that did it,' added Spit.

'No way,' said Alex. 'Think about it – we're the most popular team at the Academy. We've got loads of supporters who want to join the celebrations. No one will be able to blame us – it could have been any of them.'

'It would be cool to have the fountain going in our team colours,' admitted Inchy, pursing his lips thoughtfully.

'And it can't really do any harm,' agreed Cherry.

Spit grimaced. 'You're all nuts. Gabriel will go absolutely *mental*!'

Alex just grinned, and promptly emptied his bottle into the pond.

'Well, that didn't do much, did it?' said House, crestfallen.

The water was slowly turning a pale, unimpressive pink.

'Hang on, mate,' replied Alex, 'That's just Phase One of this particular master plan.' He turned to Cherry. 'How good are you with that bow?'

'Good enough,' said Cherry confidently.

Alex pointed to a large brass button on a wall some distance off.

'Reckon you could hit that from here?'

'You've got to be kidding,' said Spit. 'Cherry couldn't hit her own foot, never mind something that far away.'

'I've been practising!' Cherry protested.

'Whatever.'

'What's the button for, anyway?' asked Inchy.

'It turns on the fountain,' said Alex. 'But it's right under Gabriel's window – impossible to sneak up to without being seen. But if Cherry can hit it from here, we can set the fountain going and no one will have a clue who started it!'

A slow grin spread across House's wide face. 'Genius!'

Cherry fitted an arrow to her bow.

'We do this and we run, OK?' she said, raising the bow and taking aim. The gang held their breath.

With a *twang* from Cherry's bow, the arrow flew across the garden, missed the button by a mile, clattered against the window of Gabriel's office – and ricocheted right back at them.

Alex sidestepped to his left, as if dodging a defender. Spit flung himself to the right. Cherry ducked as the arrow whizzed over her head, taking her cap with it. Inchy spread his wings and soared up out of danger. In a flash, the whole team had taken perfect evasive action.

Except House.

The next few seconds seemed to play out in slow motion. Trying to avoid the flying arrow, House fell backwards, tripped over Cherry, staggered forward, stumbled over the crouching figure of Alex, lost his footing and . . .

SPLASH!

A plume of bright red water soared into the sky. When the spray cleared, House was sitting in the middle of the pond, soaked. And stained red from top to toe. For a moment, Alex thought about laughing. Then he heard The Voice booming out across the garden.

'What in Heaven is going on out there?'

'Quick!' Alex yelled to House. 'Get out! Gabriel's coming!'

House tried to pull himself up, but the bottom of the fountain was slippery with red slime. In the distance, a tall figure in snow-white robes was striding across the lawn, getting closer by the second.

'Hurry!' shouted Cherry. 'Or we're all for it!'

Desperately, House pulled himself to the edge of the fountain and climbed out on to the side, scattering crimson drops behind him. For a second, it looked like he was going to make it. Then his feet slid from under him and, arms windmilling madly, he fell backwards with another titanic splash that emptied the fountain – all over the white-robed figure, who was now quite clearly recognizable as Head Angel Gabriel.

As Cherry, Inchy and Spit fled, Alex stared, aghast. How could it all have gone so wrong? It was time to get out of there. He leapt into the air, but before he had gone more than three wingbeats, Alex felt a hand – old, calloused and extraordinarily strong – grip his ankle, stopping him dead. As he hung there in mid-air, a quiet voice, deep as a well, whispered one word into his ear.

'*Gotcha!*'

The hallway ran through the centre of Cloud Nine Academy. It was very long, very dark and very cold, and ended in an enormous door. It was the kind of door that, if you found yourself standing in front of it, meant you were almost certainly in a lot of trouble.

Alex, Spit, Cherry, Inchy and Big House knew the door very well indeed. Hardly a week went by without the gang ending up waiting outside it for a telling-off from the Head Angel. Usually because one of Alex's 'foolproof' plans hadn't turned out to be quite so foolproof as he'd thought.

Alex leaned back against the wall and smiled at his four friends. None of them smiled back.

Spit spoke first.

'It wasn't my idea to put dye in the fountain,' he said, his dark eyes fixed on Alex.

'No, it was definitely mine,' Alex grinned back. 'I just didn't think Gabriel would be so upset.'

'You didn't think he'd get upset?' said Spit. 'Old Grumpy Gabs?'

Alex laughed. No one else joined in.

Cherry spoke up, her naturally red hair blazing like fire.

'So why are we all here, then, if it's your fault?' She sighed. 'You're supposed to be training to be an Archangel – one of the leaders of Heaven. Some leader you are – you're always getting us into trouble.'

'*Big* trouble,' said House gloomily, shoving his unnaturally red hands deep into his pockets. 'This could mean big, big trouble.'

Alex looked across at his best friend, wondering how anything could ever worry him. He was at least a head taller than the rest of the gang, well built and unusually strong.

House slumped moodily back against the wall. Unfortunately, he slumped much further than he'd intended, and ended up tumbling to the ground and sitting squarely on top of Inchy.

'Oi! Watch out!' squeaked Inchy from underneath House's bulky frame.

'All you ever do, *Bungalow*,' said Spit insultingly, 'is walk into things and knock stuff over. Is there a day that goes by without you breaking something? We wouldn't even be here if you hadn't fallen into the fountain!'

'Leave it, Spit,' said Alex, stepping in, 'unless you want House to *see* red too and squash you into a ball and boot you down the hall.'

Alex eyeballed Spit, who backed off, muttering to himself. Then, with a shrug of his shoulders, Alex extended his wings. They weren't fully grown quite yet, but they were certainly big enough for flying, which, thought Alex, was easily the best bit about being an angel. With a jump, he went to hover by the shiny gold sign screwed to the door. On it were three words – *Head Angel: Shush!* A small halo shone above the 'A'.

From his vantage point, Alex watched as House scrambled up from the floor, picked Inchy up with one hand and plopped him back on to his feet.

'Sorry, Inchy,' said House. 'I must've missed the wall.'

''S'all right,' said Inchy, checking his own wings and picking up his bent glasses. 'I mean, a wall's so easy to miss, isn't it?'

Checking that the door to Gabriel's office was firmly closed, Alex did a quick loop-the-loop.

Cherry sighed. 'Alex, you know you're not supposed to fly in the corridors.'

'So what?'

'So we're in enough trouble already. Come down.'

'But there aren't any teachers about,' replied Alex, turning over to hover upside down. 'Relax.'

'Alex,' said Cherry, pulling out an arrow. 'If your feet aren't on the ground in three seconds, I'm going to fire one of these at you and make you fall in love with a donkey. Again.'

The previous week, Alex had used a permanent marker pen to draw a beard on Cherry's face while she was asleep. At the time, it had been really funny, but Cherry had got her revenge by shooting Alex with one of her Arrows of Love while he was grooming Gabriel's pet donkey. Alex couldn't remember exactly what had happened next, but it had certainly involved a rather horrible hairy kiss and some very bad breath indeed.

'You're not actually allowed to fire that at a person, you know,' he said, nodding at the bow. 'You have to be a fully qualified Cherub.'

Alex suddenly found himself staring down the length of a drawn arrow.

'Try me,' said Cherry. 'Same place as last time, OK?'

Alex's hands instinctively covered his bottom.

'Fine,' he muttered, dropping to the ground. 'I was just having some fun.'

'Like you were with the fountain?' smirked Spit.

'I thought it would be a giggle. How was I to know that Gabriel would come into the garden?'

Cherry lowered her bow.

'I reckon we vote for a new captain,' she said. 'You're rubbish, Alex.'

'Oh, come on,' protested Alex. 'We have fun, don't we? More fun than any of the other teams in the league. That's why Gabriel's got it in for us — he doesn't like anyone to have fun.

'He didn't look very happy at all,' said House.

'No,' replied Inchy. 'But then I don't think he was really expecting to have red dye sprayed all over his nice, freshly ironed, snow-white Archangel outfit.'

'At least I'm red all over. He looked like a huge raspberry ripple ice cream,' said House absently. His tummy gave a loud rumble at the thought.

'Inchy's got a point, Alex,' said Cherry. 'Do you ever think before you act?'

'It's not an act,' said Alex. 'I'm just naturally this talented. Oh, and good-looking, but that goes without saying.'

'Then why do you always say it?' asked Cherry.

'Because sometimes you need reminding.'

Cherry opened her mouth to reply, but was interrupted by the sound of a loud cough from the other side of the door. It was the kind of cough used by someone getting ready to say lots of things, none of them very nice. The gang braced themselves, but the door stayed firmly shut.

After a moment, Alex broke the silence. 'Anyway, I'm sure we've got nothing to worry about. Gabriel's harmless, really,' he whispered. 'He just likes everyone to think he's terrifying. Actually, he's a big softy.'

None of the gang looked convinced.

'Surely you've heard the stories, though?' said Spit, equally quietly.

'Stories? What stories?' said House nervously.

'Don't worry, mate,' said Alex, putting his arm almost round House's broad shoulders. 'Spit's just trying to wind you up, aren't you, Spit?'

Alex glared at Spit, trying to silence him.

'You mean the stories about what he did before he took over Cloud Nine Academy?' asked Inchy, wiping his glasses clean with his shirt.

'They're just rumours,' said Cherry. 'No one believes them.'

'What rumours?' said House. 'What's everyone talking about?'

'Let's just say,' murmured Spit, leaning closer to House, 'it's a good job we're not demons.'

'Why?' said House. 'What are you on about? What's any of this got to do with demons?'

'Nothing. Nothing at all,' said Spit innocently, although he sounded as if he was enjoying scaring House.

'Then why don't you shut up?' said Cherry.

'It's not just rumours.'

Everyone turned to listen to Inchy.

'There are books in the library, really old ones that most people don't bother to read. I was researching a project about how angels can use something called chameleon clothing to stay invisible on Earth. It's amazing stuff! It changes to look exactly like whatever's around you, so you're impossible to see. How cool is that? I don't think we get to try it until –'

'Inchy!' interrupted Cherry. 'Get on with it!'

'Oh yeah, sorry.' Inchy pushed his glasses back up his nose and continued. 'Anyway, I went into this really dark bit of the library I'd never been into before. There was this section called "The War". The books were huge, some too big to lift. But I managed to open one. It was all about Gabriel.'

'What about him?' asked Alex. 'What did it say?'

Inchy went quiet.

'Inch?' prompted House.

'To cut a long story short,' said Inchy with a heavy sigh, 'it basically said that no one kicks butt like Gabriel.'

'Well, I don't know about you guys, but that's really cheered me up,' said Spit sarcastically.

'Look,' said Alex, turning to face the whole of his gang, 'I'll say it was all my idea. I'll tell Gabriel that –'

But they never got to hear what Alex was going to say.

A sharp click cut the conversation dead and then, silent as fog, the door to Gabriel's office swung ominously open.

2
Kicked Out

Alex opened his eyes to inky darkness. He lay still for a moment, trying to get his bearings. His head felt fuzzy, as if he had just woken up. Which was odd, because he didn't remember going to sleep. He sat up – and bumped his head on something directly above him. A bunk bed. He was in a bunk bed. For a moment, Alex relaxed. Perhaps the whole disaster at the fountain had just been a bad dream. Then he remembered. He didn't have a bunk bed.

Alex rubbed his eyes and allowed them to adjust to the dark. Soon some shapes started to form in front of him, but he couldn't make out exactly what they were. Cautiously, he whispered, 'House? You there?'

A voice called out, 'Who's that? Who's there? Where am I?'

'House?'

'Alex?'

A scuffling sound came from the top bunk. It was followed by a large shape falling through the air with a soft *whoosh*.

'Umph!'

Alex looked over the side of his bed.

'House? You OK?'

'I'm fine,' said House from the floor. 'Where are we?'

Another voice answered from the dark.

'We're in big, BIG trouble, that's where.'

'Cherry?' called Alex. 'That you?'

'Of course it's me!'

'I'm here too,' sighed Spit from somewhere else in the dark.

'And me,' said Inchy.

'The whole team's here?' asked Alex. 'What's going on? What is this place?'

The darkness cracked into a flood of white. Spit stood there with his hand on the light switch.

'I think the more relevant question would be "*Where* is this place?"'

Alex stood up and looked around the room. Three metal bunk beds stood in a row against one wall. Opposite these were some old bits of furniture, including a battered-looking wardrobe, a bookcase filled with encyclopedias, a chest of drawers with all the knobs replaced with wine bottle corks, and two hard wooden chairs that looked as if they were being held together with string. At one end of the room hung some huge, thick, patchwork curtains, and at the other stood a door.

Nobody spoke. For a minute, Alex thought the others were all dumbstruck by their strange surroundings. Then he realized that they were all staring at him.

'What?'

The rest of the gang continued to stare at Alex, shock etched in their faces.

'What is it?'

House cleared his throat nervously.

'Er, Alex, mate — where are your wings?'

'What do you mean? They're here, where they always are.'

Alex flexed his shoulders, expecting his

handsome snowy wings to snap out behind him. Nothing happened.

'Our wings!' he shouted, pointing at the others. 'We haven't got our wings! None of us have; they're gone!'

The rest of the gang looked at each other, each of them feeling round their backs for the tell-tale tickle of feathers. Nothing.

'Impossible,' said Spit. 'We're angels! We have to have wings!'

'Well, we haven't got them any more,' said Cherry ominously. 'And I reckon we all know whose fault it is.'

Everyone turned to stare at Alex.

'But I told Gabriel,' spluttered Alex. 'You heard me. I said it was my idea, that it was all my fault.'

'Yes, indeed,' said Spit. 'And that was just before he said something about teaching us a lesson we'd never forget, wasn't it?'

A sound of curtains being pulled open drew everyone's attention.

'Guys,' Inchy said, his voice solemn, 'we're on Earth.'

The gang looked through the window, stunned into silence.

'This gives a whole new meaning to being grounded,' quipped Alex.

No one laughed.

'Are you sure it's Earth?' asked House. 'I mean, it doesn't look that much different to Heaven, does it?'

The view outside was of fields and trees and rain dancing down the windowpane.

'Except for that.'

Inchy nodded at an aeroplane slicing across the sky.

'And that,' said Cherry, pointing at some litter rolling by in the wind.

'And me,' came a voice from behind them.

The gang turned.

At the far end of the room, standing at the now open door, was an old man. He was wearing a very well-tailored, if rather old, tweed suit, a blue shirt, a red tie and very polished brown shoes. A row of medals shone brightly on the left side of his chest and he was leaning heavily on a cane.

Alex, as team captain and gang leader, was the first to speak.

'Hi,' he said. 'What's going on?'

'You have been sent down,' said the old man in a clipped, military-sounding voice.

'What? We're in prison?' said Cherry. 'We can't be. We didn't do anything. Well, nothing really bad. And we're too little for prison!'

'No,' replied the old man, 'this is not prison. This is number 92 Eccles Road – in the town of Green Hill, Sussex.'

'But why have we been sent here?' asked Alex.

'You have some lessons to learn,' said the old man. 'And, on the orders of Head Angel Gabriel, you are going to learn them here with me.'

From the tone of the old man's voice, Alex guessed that he wasn't much happier about the prospect than they were.

Alex turned back to the gang and winked.

'So you're in charge of us?'

'Yes. Command has been given to me.'

'But you're just an old man,' said Alex. 'I mean, if we wanted to escape, what could you do about it? Come on, guys!'

And with that, he sprang for the open door.

There was a quick, soft sound, like a cotton sheet snapping in the wind, and Alex bounced off something that felt as springy as a mattress, landing hard on his bottom.

'He's an angel,' muttered House.

'No kidding,' said Spit, his eyes wide.

Alex backed away. The old man hadn't moved, but spread out behind him were two utterly enormous wings. They were ice white and curved round the walls of the room.

The old man looked at Alex.

'I am Major Tabbris, Order of Raphael, First Class,' he said proudly, tapping one of his many decorations (a particularly enormous silver medal), 'and formerly of Special Operations. Now retired, although you wouldn't know it. Nannying a horde of screaming children is hardly my idea of a peaceful retirement.'

Alex gulped. Everyone knew about Special Ops. This elite group of angelic agents were responsible for patrolling Earth and Heaven, looking for demons and agents of the Other Side. The toughest of the tough, they weren't to be messed with.

With a flick, Tabbris's wings folded in behind him and faded to nothing.

'Now, a few ground rules –'

'Where are our wings?' interrupted Spit.

Tabbris shot Spit a glare so stern that he clamped his mouth shut.

'Rule Number One,' snapped Tabbris. 'You will only speak when you are spoken to.'

He turned and headed for the door.

'Breakfast is in the kitchen. I expect you all to be there, washed, dressed and sitting at the table in ten minutes. You have a busy day ahead of you.'

A question darted into Cherry's mind and she spoke before she could stop herself.

'What about our friends back in Heaven? Do they know what's happening to us?'

Tabbris turned.

'Gabriel will keep them informed on a need-to-know basis. Breakfast is now in nine minutes.'

And with that, Tabbris disappeared through the door, leaving the gang to wonder just what – quite literally – on Earth Alex had landed them in.

'What is it?' asked Inchy, poking his spoon into the bowl sitting in front of him. It was filled with a grey, steaming mush.

'It looks like sick,' said Cherry.

'Porridge,' said Tabbris from the end of the table. 'Eat it; you will all need your energy today.'

Alex shrugged and took a mouthful.

'Yuck! It tastes salty. What's in it?'

'Salt is in it,' said Tabbris. 'This is porridge the way it is supposed to be made, as I discovered on a mission in the Highlands of Scotland five hundred years ago.'

'Do you always eat this for breakfast?' asked Cherry.

'No,' replied Tabbris. 'But this is a special occasion. Now, chores . . .'

The gang turned from their salty porridge and stared at the old angel.

'What do you mean by "chores"?' asked Alex, dreading that an already bad day was about to get a whole lot worse.

'This house,' replied Tabbris, 'as you have no doubt realized, is exceptionally ordered and tidy. It is your job to keep it that way. I don't like mess. I don't like things not being in their proper place. I don't like knives in the fork drawer.'

Tabbris stood up and placed a thick roll of paper on the table, along with a bucket containing soap, polish and a selection of brushes and cloths.

'These are your chores,' he said. 'I would read them out, but that would be wasting valuable scrubbing time. Any questions?'

Alex put his hand in the air.

'Yes?'

'Are you mad in the head?'

The rest of the gang shouted in unison, 'Shut up!'

'What?' Alex looked hurt.

'You just can't keep your mouth shut, can you?' complained Spit.

'I will be reporting your behaviour back to Gabriel at the end of every week,' continued Tabbris, as if nobody had spoken. 'When I think you have learned to behave more like angels than animals, I will recommend that you be allowed to return to Cloud Nine, but not before. If there are no more questions, I will leave you to it,' said Tabbris. 'Lunch today will be at twelve o'clock sharp. Tea at six. Bed at eight.'

'Bed at eight?' muttered House. 'I haven't gone to bed at eight since I was, well, eight.'

'You will need a good night's sleep in preparation for tomorrow,' said Tabbris, his pencil-thin moustache twitching in what might have been a smirk.

'Do we dare ask why?' enquired Spit.

Tabbris was at the kitchen door.

'As you are now on Earth,' he said, 'you will

have to fit in with human children. Do the things they do. One of those things is school. Good day!'

Cherry picked up the list of chores. It unrolled along the length of the table and off the other end, on to the floor.

'We'll never finish all these,' she groaned, picking up a moth-eaten old duster.

But none of the others were listening. They were staring at the empty doorway through which Tabbris had vanished.

'School,' said Inchy.

'On Earth,' said Spit.

'With humans,' said House.

'Pants,' said Alex.

3
Mr Dante

'I ache all over,' moaned Big House as the gang trooped out of the front door towards school the following morning.

'I ache all under and all over,' sighed Inchy. 'It's no wonder Tabbris is retired; he's completely mad.'

'Completely mad and completely in charge,' said Cherry. 'And it's completely your fault, Alex.'

Alex looked at his friends. Behind them towered the old house they now had to call home; a home on planet Earth they shared with an insane old angel who put salt on his porridge.

'How many more times can I say I'm sorry?'

'Try a million,' said Spit. 'Then times that by twenty. And that's just for these uniforms.'

Alex looked at what they were all wearing: scratchy grey nylon shirts, grey-and-white-striped ties, thick grey jumpers and itchy grey trousers. As a finishing touch, each of them was carrying a shiny brown leather satchel – they looked about as uncool as it was possible to look. He wasn't so sure that twenty million sorries would be enough.

'What's school on Earth actually like, anyway?' asked House. 'I mean, we go to Cloud Nine Academy, don't we? That's a school and it's not too bad.'

'Well,' said Inchy, pushing his glasses up his nose, 'for a start, there're going to be no flying lessons.'

'No way!' blurted House.

'Humans can't fly,' said Inchy, 'everyone knows that. And anyway, we haven't got our wings.'

'Tell us something we don't know,' grouched Cherry.

'OK,' said Inchy, 'how about this: on Earth, teachers are allowed to lock bad children in boxes filled with worms.'

'You're joking!' said House, eyes wide with horror.

'You're so gullible,' smiled Inchy, but nobody felt much like laughing.

House opened his mouth to reply, but Spit got there first.

'Look,' he said, pointing. 'The school.'

'Big, big trouble,' muttered House.

'You said that yesterday,' said Alex.

'And I was right. Just look at that place.'

Alex was looking at it and even he couldn't conjure up a smile. He'd never seen anywhere like it. The only school he'd ever known was Cloud Nine Academy, and that was one of the most beautiful buildings in Heaven: all shiny gold, white marble and pristine gardens. This place looked like it was built of corroded metal and cold granite, held together by overgrown weeds.

The school gate, towering between two enormous stone pillars, looked like it had turned entirely to rust, the metal bars twisting into each other like brambles. Behind the gate, laid out like an enormous grey carpet, was the playground. It was dotted with scummy puddles, and chipped and scuffed at the edges, crumbling like a stale biscuit. Off to the side was a sad-looking school field, with three swampy football pitches marked out. And beyond the playground stood the school itself – a vast brick building that seemed to be built of shadows and dust. Tiny, slit-like windows stared down from the walls, as if they were spying on the screaming children in the playground, and the high slate roof seemed to be home to about a thousand crows.

'I didn't think we had to learn about Hell until Sixth Form,' said Spit. 'But it looks like we've been sent on a field trip.'

'Why's everyone looking at us?' asked Cherry, as hundreds of pairs of eyes followed them.

The gang had just walked through the school gates, and the raging torrent of noise that had been echoing around the playground had fallen silent.

'They've probably never seen angels before,' answered House.

'We don't look like angels, remember?' said Alex.

'Look!' hissed Inchy. 'Someone's coming over.'

Alex looked and saw three very tall, very slim and very attractive girls walking towards them.

'Perhaps this won't be too bad after all,' he said, nudging Spit.

When the girls arrived, the tallest and prettiest of them spoke first.

'You're new,' she said.

'I'm Cherry,' said Cherry, holding out her hand and smiling. 'Pleased to meet you.'

'Do you think I'm stupid?' asked the girl.

'No,' said Cherry, her face a mask of confusion.

'Yeah,' said one of the other girls, 'are you saying she's stupid?'

'No,' said Cherry again, 'I don't even know you.'

'So are you saying that, if you did know her, you'd say she was stupid?' asked the other girl.

Cherry didn't reply.

'We don't touch new kids,' said the first girl. 'We don't want to catch whatever it is you've got.'

'Like what?' asked Cherry indignantly.

'Like excess stomach rolls,' said the girl, pointedly patting down her skinny frame.

The other girls giggled.

'*What* did you say?' asked Cherry, her eyes blazing.

Alex stepped in.

'I'm Alex,' he said. 'And you are . . .?'

But the girls just turned and strutted off back across the playground, giggling.

'How dare she judge me on how I look,' muttered Cherry. 'If I had my bow, I'd –'

'Don't worry about it,' soothed Inchy. 'She's probably just trying to make herself look important in front of everyone.'

'Always trying to see both sides, aren't you?' said Cherry.

Inchy shrugged.

'That's what a Voice of Reason Angel is supposed to do – give a balanced view of things so that people don't make rash decisions.'

'Right,' said Alex, glancing at Tabbris's list of instructions. 'Apparently we've got to go to registration. Come on.'

'Nice bags!' came a voice from the crowd as the gang walked across the playground.

'New kids, puke kids!' came another.

'Why's everyone being nasty?' mumbled House. 'They don't even know us.'

'Ignore it,' said Alex, just as Inchy walked straight into someone.

'Oi! Watch where you're goin', stink face.'

'Sorry,' said Inchy, stepping back to see a large, greasy-haired, grubby-looking boy in front of him. His sleeves were rolled up and he was chewing a lollipop stick. Four similarly sized lads stood behind him, all scowling.

'Sorry?' said the first boy. 'You fink that's good enough, do ya, titch?'

Inchy didn't reply.

'He's ignoring you, Jackson,' said another boy.

'Now that's not very polite, is it? I fink you'll 'ave to be punished,' said the boy called Jackson. 'Grab 'im, lads!'

Alex found himself pushed out of the way as Jackson's cronies rushed forward and grabbed Inchy, pinning him to the ground.

'Right!' said Jackson, with an unpleasant leer. 'Time for a toilet flushin'!'

It was then that House stepped in.

'I think you should leave him alone.'

'I'd listen to him if I were you,' said Alex.

Jackson turned and walked towards House

until his spotty nose was almost touching House's.

'An' who's going to make me?'

House simply stared back, his face dead calm.

'Thought so,' said Jackson. 'All mouth an' no action. Come on, lads, let's soak the little drip.'

Alex knew that he really ought to step in before House did anything silly. But he didn't. He recognized that the gang couldn't afford to get labelled as prime targets for bullies on their first day. So instead he just grinned as he watched what happened next, more than a little thankful that House was on his side.

Jackson had only taken two steps towards Inchy before House had lifted the boy into the air by his ankles and started swinging him from left to right, like the pendulum on a clock. The boy's head barely missed the ground.

'Gerroff!' screamed Jackson. 'Put me down or you're dead, you hear me? *Dead!*'

Alex nodded at Spit and they both turned to the boys holding Inchy.

'Let him go,' said Alex. 'Or he lets your friend go.'

Jackson yelled out as House swung him higher. Spit arched an eyebrow.

'Well?'

As one, the gang let go of Inchy and backed off.

'You can put him down now,' said Alex to House. 'I think he's probably had enough.'

House flipped Jackson the right way up and dumped him into a nearby puddle.

'You'll pay for this,' he spluttered, staggering dizzily away. 'Just you wait; you'll all pay.'

'I didn't know you had it in you,' said Spit, patting House on the back.

'I'm training to be a Guardian Angel, remember?'

Spit looked at him.

'And you learned all about swinging people around by their feet in lessons, did you?'

House grinned.

'Nah. I made that bit up all by myself.'

'You know,' said Alex, grabbing House round the shoulders as they sauntered into the building, 'perhaps this human school lark won't be too bad after all . . .'

'Do you think these pipes are supposed to make those sounds?'

Spit winced as a large duct above them let out

a barrage of clanks and wheezes, releasing a choking cloud of dust into the air.

The inside of the school was, if possible, even more ramshackle than the outside, filled with long damp corridors, broken doors and cracked windows, as well as the rusty pipes that banged and rattled incessantly.

It had been a boring day of meeting new teachers, collecting books and getting lost in the shabby hallways. The only good thing had been that the school five-a-side football season was about to start and they had all been able to sign up to play together.

'What've we got now?' asked House as the gang arrived outside a classroom for their last lesson of the day.

'Whatever it is, I hope we get out of it before this place falls down,' said Inchy.

'Or melts,' added Cherry. 'It's so warm! What's that about? And this room's even hotter.'

'It's geography, I think,' said Alex. 'Perhaps we're studying global warming!'

No one laughed.

'Well, from what I've heard today,' continued Alex, 'it should be interesting, anyway.'

'Why?' asked Spit.

'Well, apparently the teacher's a bit nuts.'

'Define "nuts".'

'Nuts is nuts, isn't it? I think he's called Dante.'

'That's *Mr* Dante,' came a deep voice, 'but I suggest you call me "sir".'

Alex turned. The voice had come from a tall man at the front of the classroom. He looked, thought Alex, like someone built entirely out of burnt matchsticks: terribly thin and strangely twisted. His cheeks were sunken pools of grey, his eyes dark holes. Alex knew he was staring, but there was something about the teacher that meant he couldn't turn away.

'He heard you call him nuts,' whispered Inchy.

'You think I don't know that?' hissed Alex.

Dante curled a finger on his right hand, beckoning Alex towards him.

'Can I just sit down?' asked Alex, as the rest of the gang slipped into the room and quickly found themselves some seats.

'In every way, no,' said Dante in a voice like thick oil oozing from a walking scarecrow.

Alex swallowed hard and walked across to the front of the classroom. When he reached Dante's side, he was struck by a strange acrid smell in the air, as if something burning had been put out with water.

'Name?' asked Dante, leaning in close to him.

'Alex,' said Alex.

'Surname?'

Surname? thought Alex frantically. *I haven't got one!*

'Well?'

'Er, it's, um . . . Cloud.'

'Cloud?'

'Yeah, that's it. Alex Cloud. Sir.'

'Very well,' said Dante. 'A quick test, Cloud.' He pulled down a map from an old-fashioned roller attached to the ceiling. 'Where is Bolivia?'

Alex had never even heard of Bolivia.

'Um, is it in France?'

Dante sighed.

'The Cape of Good Hope?'

Alex was silent.

With a tug, Dante sent the map rattling back up to the ceiling. He handed Alex a piece of chalk.

'What's this?' asked Alex.

'It's chalk, you ignorant child. Used for writing

on the blackboard.' Dante pointed with one clawlike finger.

'You're still using a *blackboard*?' Alex couldn't believe it. 'What is this – the Dark Ages?'

Dante smiled thinly. 'Spell "globalization".'

Alex glanced at his friends.

'It's not fair . . . We're new and . . .'

His voice trailed off.

'Life isn't fair, I'm afraid, Cloud, so you'd better just get used to it. Now, draw a cross section of a river.'

Alex didn't move.

'Oh dear,' sneered Dante. 'Evans!'

Without a word, a terrified-looking boy darted to the front of the classroom, wrote "Globalization" on the board, drew a cross section of a river, then ran back to his desk.

Dante leaned down towards Alex.

'I've already heard about the trouble in the playground this morning, Cloud. I know your sort well . . .'

Alex doubted that very much, but managed to bite his tongue for once.

'. . . and if this is the best you can do, I think you might find my lessons something of a struggle. So I suggest you keep your head down and your mouth shut – you don't want to get on the wrong side of me.'

Before Alex could reply, Dante turned and strode off to his desk. Scurrying to the back of the classroom, Alex sat down next to House.

'Great,' he muttered. 'This is just what we need – the teacher from Hell . . .'

4
Team Spirit

'I don't care what it takes,' said House, 'but I want out of this place. It sucks.'

'Too right,' said Cherry. 'How long do you think Gabriel's going to keep us here?'

'Until we're as old as Tabbris and twice as loopy,' replied Spit darkly.

It was Friday afternoon. The week had flown by about as quickly as a dead chicken, and the gang were making their way towards the school fields, where Alex had booked one of the football pitches so they could have a knockabout. Just because they were stuck on Earth, at one of the worst schools in history, that didn't mean they couldn't do *something* they enjoyed.

House kicked moodily at the ball and it flew off into the distance, narrowly missing Cherry's head.

'Watch it!'

'Sorry,' said House, and ran off after the ball.

'I'm amazed we ever won a match with him playing,' sighed Spit.

'And I'm amazed we still like you hanging around with us,' said Alex. 'I mean, do you practise at being so nice or does it just come naturally?'

Spit sneered and strolled off.

'Why's he being like that?' asked Cherry, trotting up beside Alex. 'He's always grumpy, I know, but since we got here, he's been getting worse and worse.'

Alex shrugged as Inchy and House joined them. 'Earth life doesn't agree with him. I think he's still cross about being sent down.'

'Well, we're all in the same boat,' snapped Cherry. 'Besides, he may be in the High Flyers programme like you are, Alex, but it's not like he actually *wants* to be an Archangel. So it doesn't matter if he's been sent down. Not like it does for you, anyway.'

Alex grimaced at the reminder. He'd always been unlikely to make Archangel – only the very best of the High Flyers managed that – but he'd always harboured a secret hope that he might. Getting suspended from Cloud Nine had probably scuppered any chance he'd had, though.

'Right,' said Alex, trying to forget his troubles for a moment. 'With our unbeaten record, winning this school league should be a doddle, but it can't hurt to get some practice in. We don't want to lose our championship skills now, do we?'

'Do you think it'll be any different playing here?' asked Cherry. 'I mean, we haven't got our wings for a start.'

'Well,' said Inchy, 'that just means we're not going to be able to use high defence and aerial attack. I'm sure we'll be fine.'

'So let's get on with it, then!' shouted Alex, clapping his hands. 'We'll play two-on-two, one in goal. OK?'

'Well, it's a plan,' shrugged Spit.

'I'll go in goal; Inchy, you're with Cherry; House, you're with Spit.'

Spit gave a long-suffering sigh.

'Get used to it,' said Alex. 'We play as a team, we win as a team, get it? Right, let's go!'

With that, House kicked off.

It didn't take anyone long to realize that they weren't very good.

'I'm here!' yelled Cherry as the ball flew miles past her for the seventh time. 'Not over there!'

'I know!' retorted Inchy. 'But the ball just feels different.'

'Different?' said Spit. 'It's like it weighs three times as much as normal.'

'That's because it does,' said Alex. 'Earth gravity's different.'

'Look out!' came a cry and the ball whizzed between them, pinged off the crossbar and bounced away into the distance.

'Sorry,' called House, jogging past.

'The ball's heavier, so he's kicking it even harder,' said Cherry, shaking her head. 'We'll be lucky to get off the pitch alive if he keeps playing like that.'

'What's the score?' asked Alex, trying to keep the team motivated.

'Two all,' said Spit.

House came charging back, dribbling the ball with an expression of furious concentration on his face.

'Aerial it!' yelled Alex, without thinking. The

aerial attack had been one of the team's most successful plays in the Cloud Nine championships.

Immediately, House chipped the ball high in the air and charged towards Spit.

'Spring me!' he shouted.

Automatically, Spit crouched down, joining his hands together ready to give House a leg up into the air, where he could smack the ball back down into the goal. House, his eye on the ball, thundered towards him, put his foot firmly into Spit's linked hands, spread his wings and –

CRASH!

Without his wings to lift him, Big House's enormous bulk flattened the dark-haired angel into the mud. House himself was sent cartwheeling along the ground, knocking Alex, Cherry and Inchy over like ninepins, before thumping into a goalpost.

As they lay dazed, the sound of hysterical laughter split the air.

'Who's that?' snarled Cherry.

House turned to see. 'They look a bit familiar,' he said morosely.

Sure enough, Jackson and the gang of bullies who'd pushed Inchy around on Monday morning stood on the sidelines, doubled up with laughter. One of the boys retrieved the ball, flicked it up on to his knee and bounced it half a dozen times, before heading it high, controlling it on his chest and whacking it into the back of the net.

'Just you wait, losers. We're The Black Crows – and you're playing us in two weeks!'

With a rude gesture, the Black Crows sauntered off.

'They're going to murder us, aren't they?' said Inchy.

'There's nothing to be afraid of,' replied House. 'I'll play in defence.'

'I couldn't think of anywhere better to field a Guardian Angel,' smiled Alex. 'Anyway, if we're not playing them for two weeks, that's more than long enough to get used to Earth conditions.'

'You reckon?' said Spit, his hands thrust deep in the pockets of his shorts. 'Not only are they obviously better than us, but we've got House on our side. That's enough to guarantee defeat.'

'We've got to think positively.'

'Right,' retorted Spit, as the gang trooped despondently back to the changing rooms with the laughter of their opponents still ringing in their ears. 'Think positively. That'll help.'

5
Turning Up the Heat

Back at Cloud Nine, weekends had been fun. There were all sorts of activities that the gang were involved in. Cherry enjoyed her archery club, even if she was by far the worst shot out of all the Cherubs in her year; Inchy usually played chess or some other intelligent game; Alex and Spit usually found time for a one-on-one kickabout; and House looked forward to Sunday lunch.

This weekend had been rather different.

Saturday morning was spent polishing every single one of the 204 brass picture frames that decorated the walls of Tabbris's house. At lunchtime, Tabbris inspected their work. Unimpressed by their polishing standards, he made the gang clean 117 of them again in the afternoon.

On Sunday, Alex tried to lighten the atmosphere at breakfast by pretending to find a frog in his porridge. Unfortunately, Tabbris didn't see the funny side. Alex spent the rest of the day polishing the picture frames for a *third* time, while the rest of the gang washed and peeled vegetables for a cheerless dinner of cabbage and swede, which had an unpleasant effect on Big House's digestive system – an effect that kept the gang awake most of the night, hanging out of the window in a desperate bid for fresh air.

Now it was Monday already, and the weekend felt like it had never really started. And all the horrible tasks and chores paled into insignificance compared to the prospect of another day at human school.

Capped off by geography with Mr Dante.

Alex scratched his head. 'I swear it's even hotter in here today.'

'Why don't weekends last forever?' asked Cherry. 'It's as if we're given loads of time to do the stuff we hate, and no time at all to do the stuff we love. It's very unfair.'

Spit leaned forward over his desk.

'It's like what Dante said last week: life isn't fair, so we'd better get used to it.'

'Big fan of Dante's now, are you?' asked Cherry.

'No, but he's got a point.'

'I agree,' said Inchy. 'If life was easy all the time we wouldn't appreciate the really cool bits, would we? It'd all be the same. How boring's that?'

'What's boring about everything being great?' asked House.

Alex rolled his eyes.

'What's your favourite thing in the world, House?'

'Chocolate cake. Thick, gooey, sticky chocolate cake, with thick, gooey, sticky icing.'

'Well, once you've finished drooling, imagine eating it for every meal, every day, forever.'

'What, the same cake, all the time?'

'Yep.'

'What about ice cream?'

'Nope, just the cake.'

'What about pies?'

'Just the cake, House, that's it.'

'What about –'

Alex jumped in before House could speak.

'There are no "what about"s! All you get is the cake. No ice cream, no pies, no sandwiches, no chips, no pizza, no pasta, no roast dinner. Just that cake.'

'That's rubbish!'

'Exactly,' said Spit. 'Which is why I said Dante had a point.'

'When was he talking about chocolate cake?'

Spit looked as if he was about to call House something very rude, but at that precise moment Dante strode into the room.

'Cloud! To the front, if you would be so kind.'

Alex got to his feet warily. He couldn't have done anything wrong yet – the lesson hadn't even started.

'Yes?' said Alex, arriving at the front of the classroom.

'Yes, what?'

'Yes, Mr Dante?'

Dante's smile slowly turned from a faint crease to a deep cut.

'Another little test. To see if you've learned anything yet. What is the capital of Spain?'

'Um . . .'

'Come along, Cloud. We covered this on Thursday. It shouldn't be too difficult.'

But it was. Alex's mind was blank. All he could see before him was a sea of faces, staring. Whatever he had learned the week before had disappeared from his mind. He opened his mouth to say something, but only a dry gurgle came out.

'Is that the best you can do?'

Alex couldn't say yes or no. He couldn't even nod or shake his head; he was frozen to the ground.

Dante picked something up from his desk.

'This,' he said, 'is a blackboard rubber.'

Alex looked down at Dante's hand. He was holding a dusty-looking lump of wood with a soft felt bottom.

'I use it for rubbing out mistakes, Cloud.'

Alex just stood there, unmoving.

'Are you a mistake, Cloud?'

Alex didn't know what to say.

'Well? Are you? Do I need to erase you too?'

Alex opened his mouth to say *No, I'm not a mistake, I'm Alex, and you can't rub me out*, but Dante didn't give him the chance.

Dante took the blackboard rubber and rubbed it up and down Alex's face, sending a cloud of chalk dust all over him.

Alex coughed and spat.

'He looks like a dead person!' shouted someone from the back of the class. Jackson, by the sound of it. Everyone except Big House, Inchy, Cherry and Spit laughed.

'Has that jogged your memory?' asked Dante. 'Or has everything we learned last week simply fallen from your head and on to the carpet?'

Alex rubbed his eyes, no answers in his brain.

The blackboard eraser was once again rubbed up and down his face.

'What's he got against Alex?' whispered Cherry to Inchy.

'Who knows.'

Alex looked at Dante, his face now nothing more than a white mask of chalk.

'It seems that the cat has got your tongue, Cloud.'

Alex couldn't think of anything to say that wasn't a swear word. He looked at his friends and knew none of them could help; he was completely alone.

The rest of the class just kept laughing.

Alex closed his eyes as Dante spoke again.

'It seems, Cloud, that you are indeed a mistake.'

Alex felt the blackboard rubber push into his face again. Up and down it rubbed, until he was little more than an image of a boy hidden from sight by a dusty cloud.

When Alex opened his eyes, Dante was leaning down, his eyes almost level with Alex's. His breath smelt like damp wood after a bonfire.

'This world is full of mistakes, Cloud,' he muttered, 'and they all need erasing, one by one.'

Dante's eyes caught the light and glinted.

'Back to your seat.'

Alex turned from Dante and made his way across the classroom, back to his chair. He could feel the rest of the class staring at him, laughing at him, glad it hadn't been them and hoping it never would be.

'You OK?' asked House.

Alex looked at him.

'Didn't think so.'

When the lesson finally came to an end and the bell rang, Alex was the first out of the door, quickly followed by his friends. Like Dante's classroom, the rest of the school seemed to be hotter than ever before. Above them, the pipes were bubbling and wheezing and rattling.

It took a few minutes for the gang to catch up with Alex, by which time he was already outside the school gates and heading home.

'Alex!' called Cherry, jogging up to him. 'Alex! Stop!'

Reluctantly, Alex turned to wait for the others.

'Look,' said Cherry, 'we just have to get through this, OK? Gabriel can't leave us down here forever, can he?'

'Easy for you to say,' said Alex. 'I mean, look at me!'

'It's just chalk,' observed Spit.

'But why's it me he's always getting at? What's his problem? Why doesn't he pick on anyone else? What've I done?'

They walked on in silence for a few moments.

'You know what?' said Alex, finally. 'I reckon Gabriel's put him up to it. Yeah, that's what's happened; Gabriel's had a word with Dante and told him to make my life Hell.'

'Gabriel wouldn't do that,' said Inchy. 'Angels

aren't allowed to speak to humans unless they're told to, and that's only when something really, really good is about to happen.'

'Or something really, really bad,' added Spit.

At the front door, the gang were greeted by Tabbris.

'And what happened to you?'

'I got bored of my normal uniform and figured I'd go to school as a ghost.'

Tabbris sniffed.

'Disgraceful. In my day, if anyone from Special Operations turned up on parade with their uniform in that state, they would have been court-martialled on the spot.'

'Lucky I'm not in Special Operations, then, isn't it?'

'Less of your cheek, you impertinent pup!' snapped Tabbris. 'You don't seem to realize that none of you will be going back to Heaven until I report to Gabriel that you've learned your lesson. And that certainly won't happen until you can show some respect for your elders.'

Alex groaned inwardly.

'Now, there are some things in your room for you. They were delivered earlier today. Tea at six o'clock sharp, as usual.'

Tabbris turned and stalked off without another word.

'Always so friendly,' muttered House.

'"Things"?' exclaimed Alex, looking confused. 'What's he on about?'

Spit was first into the room.

'It's just trunks. Our school trunks from Cloud Nine. Boring.'

'On the contrary!' said Alex. 'It's fantastic!'

He pulled open his trunk and started rifling through the contents, slinging pants and T-shirts in all directions.

'But that's just your clothes,' said Cherry. 'What's so exciting?'

'This,' replied Alex, pointing.

'It's the bottom of your trunk,' said Spit. 'Thrilling.'

'Well, it is, actually,' laughed Alex. 'Watch!'

He reached in and pressed one of the corners. With a *click*, the whole bottom of the trunk came loose, revealing a hidden compartment.

The gang were stunned.

'I always keep a load of stuff hidden here for use in an emergency.'

'I'm assuming Gabriel doesn't know anything about this?' asked Inchy.

'You'd better believe he doesn't!' crowed Alex, as he reached into the trunk. When he stood up again, there was something in his arms.

'I don't believe it,' said Cherry. 'It can't be . . .'

The others just stared.

'It's my back-up bow and arrows! I thought I'd lost them months ago. You mean to say you've been hiding them the whole time?'

'For use in an emergency – I'd say this qualifies!'

Alex reached in again and handed something to Inchy.

'It's my Scales of Justice!' he yelled. 'Cool or what?'

The scales were a simple length of brass with a small golden bowl hanging from a chain at each end. In the middle of the brass beam was a pivot that allowed the scales to tip left or right.

'That's all we need,' grumbled Spit. 'You weighing up everything we say or do.'

Alex's voice cut in: 'Oh yes!'

The gang turned to see what he was holding.

'My Lucky Dip! Brilliant!'

The Lucky Dip was a red cloth bag filled with all sorts of bits and bobs that Alex had managed to pick up here and there. Whenever he had used it in the past, the Lucky Dip had proved to be incredibly *un*lucky for an assortment of unsuspecting angelic teachers whom Alex had happened to fall out with.

Alex handed a large book to House.

'What's that?' asked Inchy.

'A book,' said House secretively.

'Yes, but what's it about?'

'Oh, right . . . yeah . . . well, it's the Guardian Angel training manual. It's like the ultimate guide to being one. It's got loads about training and secret moves and stuff. It's awesome.'

'Well, I doubt there's anything in there for me, is there?' said Spit. 'It's not like I have silly trinkets to carry around with me.'

'That's why I threw this in for you,' said Alex, handing Spit a large box. 'It's your favourite, I think.'

The box was filled with chocolate. And lots of it.

Alex looked around at the gang with pride. Everyone was obviously thrilled with what he'd produced from the trunk. Not such a lousy leader now, was he? For the first time since he'd got them into this mess, Alex felt a bit less guilty.

He looked again at the Lucky Dip.

'Oh, Mr Dante – now the odds are evened!'

6
True Colours

'I know Mr Dante doesn't like you,' House complained, rubbing his head, 'but I don't see why he has to throw textbooks at *me.*'

It was Wednesday, and the gang had just endured geography again. Dante had proved to be just as horrible the third time around, humiliating Cherry when she couldn't name five cities in Outer Mongolia, and giving Spit a detention for his answer that the most dangerous animal in China was the ladybird.

'He's got it in for all of us,' Alex replied as the gang trailed down the hot stuffy corridor behind

House's large and ungainly frame. 'He's as bad as Gabriel. I mean, what's the point of being a teacher if you hate kids?'

'What's the point of being a teacher, full stop?' shot back Spit, flicking a sweaty lock of dark hair out of his eyes.

There was silence as the gang mulled this difficult question over.

At the back of the group, Cherry sighed. She always pretended that she was above the boys' bickering, though she was just as likely to get into an argument as any of them. She shifted the quiver on her back. It was a pretty unusual-looking school bag, but no one had asked any awkward questions yet. Spit glanced back at her and grinned slyly.

'You can sort this out, can't you, Cherry? Just fire one of those Love Arrows at Dante, and he and Alex'll make up in no time.'

The Cherub glared at him.

'If you don't watch it, I'll make you fall in love with the next dog that walks past. We'll see how funny you are then.'

The gang crashed through a set of double doors and out into the playground. After the hot dingy corridors, it was good to be out in the fresh air. All around them gaggles of children were standing about, chatting and gossiping. The air rang with shouts of laughter. A football bounced over from a game taking place on the other side of the playground and landed at House's feet. One of the footballers waved at him to pass it back. House lined up a swing. The gang dived out of the way.

The ball cannoned off House's foot to his left, far above the heads of everyone in the playground. It bounced twice on the roof of the biology block, before disappearing out of sight.

'Oh, well done,' said Spit, clapping sarcastically as he got to his feet. 'Well done indeed. With those skills, we're just bound to win that footie match, aren't we?'

'I didn't mean to do that,' replied House.

'You couldn't have done that if you *had* wanted to,' said Alex, smiling. 'You're just naturally untalented.'

He patted House on the back.

'Come on. Me and you've got English now, haven't we? We'll see the rest of you at lunch.'

Later, as Big House stared at the whiteboard, trying to decipher the teacher's handwriting, Alex slipped a folded piece of paper in front of him.

House opened it carefully under the desk, trying not to tear it. The note read, *I have a plan.*

House groaned. This wasn't good news. Alex grinned, and gave him the thumbs up.

When the lesson ended, House tried to make a break for the canteen, but Alex grabbed him by the shoulder and led him in the other direction.

'Come on!' he hissed.

'Shouldn't we go and find the others?' tried House.

'No time. This plan won't wait.'

Alex pulled a small red bag from his pocket, wrinkles of mischief creasing the corner of his eyes.

'Oh no,' said House, putting his head in his hands, 'not the Lucky Dip . . .'

'Look,' said Alex, 'seeing as I've got it back, I may as well put it to good use. And what use could be better than getting our own back on Dante?' He opened the bag and pulled from it a reel of fishing line and some fishing weights. 'Perfect.'

With a sinking feeling in the pit of his stomach, House realized that they were heading directly for the geography teacher's office. Before he could stop him, Alex peeked through the window in the door and then slipped inside. House looked up and down the corridor. He knew that they were going to get into trouble, but if he did want to become a Guardian Angel, he couldn't desert his friend. He'd read that in the manual Alex had given him on Monday, just before he'd got on to the really interesting stuff about duffing up demons.

Alex was tying the fishing line to a latch on the window as House reluctantly entered the office. He turned and grinned at his big friend.

'I knew you wouldn't let me down.'

'Can we just get this over with and get caught?'

'Trust me – this one's foolproof.'

Alex tied a lead fishing weight to the line, and then began paying out the line across the floor. 'All we have to do is pull on this and the weight will tap against the window. Dante'll never see the fishing line. He'll think people are throwing stones against the window. It'll drive him nuts!'

'Er, and where are we going to be during all of this?'

Alex pointed at a large sofa just beside the door.

'Behind there.'

'What?'

Alex grinned again. 'But first we have to

64

prepare our escape route.' He rummaged around in the Lucky Dip for a second time. 'Bingo!' He carefully positioned the small wooden wedge on the floor, against the edge of the door frame. 'That'll keep the door ajar, so we can slip out quietly afterwards.'

'Alex, I'm really not sure about this . . .'

The sound of echoing footsteps came from the corridor outside.

'He's coming! Quick!'

The two boys barely had time to dive behind the sofa before Mr Dante strode into his office. House didn't dare to breathe. A chair creaked as the teacher sat down behind his desk, and then there was the sound of a biro scratching across a piece of paper.

His eyes shining with glee, Alex tugged on the fishing line.

Tap-tap . . .

Nothing. Alex pulled again, harder this time.

Tap-tap-tappity-tap . . .

There was a *creak*, and from behind the sofa House watched Mr Dante's shadow as it moved over towards the window.

'Who's there?' he said sharply. His voice was harsh, the sound of gravel being poured on to a huge drum. Receiving no answer, he returned to his desk, muttering under his breath.

Tap-tap-tappity-tap . . .

Alex's sides were shaking with mirth as he pulled on the line. This time there was no response from the teacher.

Tap-tap-tappity-tap . . .

Still nothing.

Tap-tap-tappity-tap . . .

A harsh and terrifying roar erupted from Mr Dante, a noise that seemed to be made of a hundred different sounds: rocks breaking into rubble; howling wind and rumbling thunder; the roar of lions and the cawing of crows. The room filled with darkness as the teacher's shadow began to shift and change on the wall behind him, moulding into the form of two giant bat-like wings. Suddenly the office felt very, very hot.

House gaped at Alex, his eyes ready to pop. Without a word, the pair of them leapt out from behind the sofa as if their legs were made of springs, and bolted through the narrowly open door. They charged out of Mr Dante's office and pelted down the deserted corridor, running until their lungs felt like bursting and they made it back to the safety of the playground.

Alex bent double, his hands on his knees, as he fought to regain his breath.

'Did . . . Did you see that?'

'More importantly, did he see us?'

'Don't think so. He'd've chased after us if he had. He was facing the window.'

House nodded in agreement, his breath coming in huge gulps.

'But . . . That was . . . Dante's a *demon*! Here in this school! What are we going to do?'

A thoughtful look crossed Alex's face.

'I don't know. But it might not all be bad news.'

'And how d'you figure that?'

'Look, if there's one dead-cert way to get back into Gabriel's good books, it's the bagging of a demon.'

House threw his hands up in the air with exasperation.

'Are you kidding me? We're not even Level One Angels. You have to be at least Level Three to take on a demon and have even a chance of surviving!'

'Maybe so,' Alex replied, smiling. 'But I have a plan . . .'

7
Undercover

'You're making it up,' said Spit. 'There's no way Dante's a demon.'

The gang were standing in the cloakroom, away from prying eyes and waggling ears. Their conversation was one they didn't want to become general knowledge. Who knows how human kids would react if they knew their geography teacher was a demon?

'Why would we lie?' said Alex through clenched teeth.

'More importantly, why were you in his office in the first place?' asked Cherry. 'You're in enough trouble with him as it is!'

'That doesn't matter now, does it?' hissed Alex. 'And anyway, if we hadn't been in there, we wouldn't have found out about Dante, would we?'

'But he can't be a demon,' said Spit. 'It must be the heating in this rubbish school sending you mad. Your brain's swelling or something. Perhaps you should go home for the rest of the day and have a lie-down.'

'I don't need to lie down,' said Alex. 'I need to get Dante.'

'The brave talk of a fool,' said Spit, shaking his head. 'How do you suggest we get him? With a big net? Or perhaps we just walk in and say, "Ah, Dante, we're actually angels and we've sussed you out. So come along quietly and we'll take you to Gabriel for a good telling-off." You're ill. Seriously.'

'Look,' said Alex, ignoring Spit and addressing the whole gang. 'Imagine what would happen if we could bag a demon. We'd be heroes! Gabriel would have to welcome us back with open arms!'

'I agree with Spit,' said Cherry. 'The heat's definitely got to you.'

As if in agreement, a *rattle, squeal, crash, gurgle* and *bang* echoed down a nearby pipe.

'It's far too dangerous,' said Inchy, holding his Scales of Justice. He touched one of the little golden bowls dangling from the scales and said, 'On this side, we've got us getting Dante. And on this side,' he touched the other bowl, 'we've got us telling Gabriel and letting him sort it out.'

Inchy had barely touched the second bowl before it plummeted towards the ground like it was made of lead.

'And what's that supposed to tell us?' asked Spit.

'That we should go to Gabriel, doofus.'

'And what will Gabriel do?' asked Alex.

'He'll send in the Guardian Angels. Special Operations,' said Inchy promptly. 'Straight in and straight out. Almost clinical, really. No humans will get hurt, no one will ever know. They're pretty cool, those Spec Ops guys.'

'I know,' said House. 'It's what I want to be when I pass my exams.'

'Gabriel won't just do that, though,' said Alex. 'He'll also claim the glory for himself, and I don't know about the rest of you, but I can't help thinking that if there's one angel who doesn't need any more glory, it's Gabriel.'

'He'd reward us, surely?' pouted Cherry.

'No, he wouldn't,' said Alex. 'He'd want to hide the fact that it was us that found out about Dante in the first place. For all we know, he might even leave us down here for good so that we could never tell people what really happened.'

The gang went silent.

'Think of it, Cherry; imagine returning home as a hero, crowds cheering, everyone asking you about how you captured the demon. They'd be telling stories about you forever – the youngest-ever demon-catching Cherub!'

'It would be pretty cool,' admitted Cherry.

'And you, House,' said Alex. 'You say you want to go into Spec Ops; well, here's your chance to really impress them!'

House nodded thoughtfully.

'What about you, Inchy? You're the one with all the brains. Don't you want to test yourself a bit, to see if you've really got what it takes? What better challenge than beating a demon?'

Inchy bit his lip, his brow furrowed. But he looked tempted.

'That leaves you, Spit. You're supposed to be

a High Flyer. Are you going to back down and be a coward instead? Nothing more than an angel who sits at home and listens to everyone talking about how Gabriel nabbed a demon you could've caught yourself? Is that really what you want?'

Spit simply stared at Alex, his eyes almost hidden behind the black hair of his fringe.

'You reckon Spec Ops would take me seriously?' asked House.

'What do you think?' replied Alex.

'I'd rather return to Cloud Nine as a hero than someone who's just learned a lesson,' said Cherry.

'What about you, Inchy? Spit?'

Inchy stuffed his hands into his pockets.

'I guess it's worth thinking about,' he said. 'I mean, it's not like we actually have to catch Dante right *now*, is it? We could just . . . find out a bit more about him, couldn't we?'

'This is insane,' said Spit. 'You know that, don't you?'

Alex nodded.

Spit sighed. 'Then count me in.'

'So, are we going to need a net?'

'What for?' asked Alex, baffled by House's earnest question.

'To catch the demon. Spit said we'd need a net.'

Alex smiled.

'No, we don't need a net. Well, not yet, anyway.'

'So what's the plan?' Cherry sounded keen to get going.

'Well, none of us studied demons very much back at Cloud Nine, so the first thing we need to do is some research – we need to know how we can recognize them, what their strengths and weaknesses are, whether they have any secret powers. That sort of thing.'

'I could do that,' chirped Inchy. 'The library's like a second home for me.'

'Cool,' said Alex. 'Meanwhile –'

'Hang on,' interrupted Spit. 'We're going to need Inchy to keep tabs on Dante and see if he's up to anything. He's the smallest and quietest, so he's the least likely to get caught.'

'But someone's got to hit the books,' complained Alex. 'We have to find out what we're dealing with.'

Spit shrugged. 'I could do it.'

'You?' Cherry frowned. 'You don't usually volunteer to do anything.'

'Yeah . . . well . . .' replied Spit awkwardly. '. . . I know how important this is,' he finished in a rush.

'Good lad!' beamed Alex. 'That's the attitude! Cherry, why don't you get some archery practice in after school. You have to admit that you need it, and *we* might need your firepower.'

Cherry bristled at the suggestion that she needed to practise, but Alex carried on regardless. 'House, I suggest you get reading that training manual of yours; if we ever needed a Guardian Angel, it's now.'

'That leaves you,' said House.

Alex grinned.

'I'm going to do what I do best – cause trouble. If Dante's always got his eye on me, he's less likely to notice that you lot are up to something.'

'So you're a decoy, then?'

'Yeah,' said Alex with a gulp. 'But it doesn't sound like much fun when you put it like that, does it?'

For the rest of the week, the gang went about their school routine as inconspicuously as possible. Not only was there the mission to prove that

Dante was indeed a demon, but the first footie match was fast approaching. The team had to practise after school every night, which meant they had to use lunch- and breaktimes for their undercover activities.

Spit spent most breaktimes in the library. He'd soon discovered that none of the books were any help, and had hopped on to the Internet instead, spending hours surfing weird and wonderful websites on Demonology. He was certainly throwing himself into the research much more willingly than Alex had expected.

Inchy was doing his best to find out what Dante got up to when he wasn't teaching. He was pretty close to being spotted a number of times, but thanks to his size and speed he always managed to duck round a corner or into a store cupboard in the nick of time.

Cherry was trying to improve her shooting, without much success. She was still haunted by the memory of the disastrous arrow she'd fired at the fountain-switch back at Cloud Nine. No true Cherub would ever shoot like that. She was practising by firing at a big heart-shaped target she'd made from cardboard and placed at the bottom of the garden at number 92. She didn't hit it very much, but by Friday she wasn't losing her arrows so often.

When House wasn't reading, he was running or doing press-ups or jumping and flipping round the garden, destroying invisible villains with deadly lightning-quick kicks and punches. At least in his mind. In reality, he was having trouble mastering the advanced techniques in the Guardian Angel manual. So far he had managed to trip over a hosepipe, smash the bird bath to smithereens and flatten a flower bed full of roses. Cherry had spent one whole evening reluctantly pulling thorns out of his bottom.

But it was Alex who had the worst time out of everyone. By far. He'd been quite looking forward to unleashing his full powers of mischief-making on Mr Dante, but he soon found that playing pranks and tricks just wasn't any fun when he was trying to get caught instead of trying to get away with it. And although Alex's attention-seeking antics succeeded in keeping Dante's attention firmly on him rather than the rest of the gang, that was most definitely a mixed blessing. It just meant he had to bear the brunt of the endless list of punishments that Dante threw at him, from blackboard-rubber dustings to hundreds and hundreds of lines. The only thing that kept him going was the thought of revenge.

'I'll get you, demon,' he muttered, as he left his third detention with Dante that week. 'You see if I don't.'

It was on Friday that the gang's hard work finally paid off.

'I've seen something,' whispered Inchy, as they gathered up their bags in the cloakroom at the end of the day. 'I followed Dante and . . . something happened.'

Alex stopped and looked at him. Inchy was pale and his eyes were wide.

'We can't talk about this here,' said Alex, looking at all the other kids milling around, collecting their coats and lunchboxes.

'We can't exactly talk about it back at the house either, though, can we?' whispered Cherry. 'If Tabbris hears what we're up to, we'll be in even deeper trouble than we already are. He'll never recommend that Gabriel should take us back. We'll probably be forced to stay here forever!'

'I've got a place we can go,' said House.

'What?' asked Alex incredulously.

'Um, I found a shed in the woods at the bottom of the garden. It's totally hidden because the wood's so overgrown. I don't think Tabbris ever goes there, or if he even knows it exists. I've been using it as, like, my base.'

'Ooh, our very own secret gang hideout,' smirked Spit.

'Shut up, Spit,' said Alex. 'It sounds perfect.'

'But won't Tabbris notice us all tramping down to it?' asked Inchy.

'No,' said House. 'Not if we cut down the side of the garden, behind all the hedges. We'll probably need to take some torches or candles or something, but it'll be all right. We can sneak out through the bedroom window.'

'Sounds good to me,' said Alex. 'Let's put this plan into action. Tonight.'

For once, bedtime arrived too slowly for everyone. Eventually, though, the gang trooped up to their room, leaving Tabbris downstairs, polishing his big silver Order of Raphael medal. The old angel was deaf in one ear and Alex reckoned that if they were quiet, he'd never notice them slipping out.

'Right,' he said, 'I'll go first. The rest of you follow, one by one.'

'Are we really going to have a secret gang hideout?' asked Spit.

'Got a problem with that?'

'No, not really,' replied Spit. 'Just seems a bit melodramatic, that's all.'

'Stay here if you want.'

'What, and miss all the fun?'

Alex made his way over to the window and opened it.

'Count to ten, then follow, one at a time, OK?'

Seconds later, he clambered out of the window and down into the garden.

It was already getting dark, even though it was only just past eight o'clock. For once, Alex was glad that Tabbris had set them such a stupidly early bedtime. The air was cool and the garden looked eerie in the half-light. Alex stood silent for a moment. Then, as quietly as possible, he made his way to the thick holly hedge that ran along one side of the garden.

Behind the hedge everything smelled damp and woody. The ground was soft, and tiny twigs and dead leaves cracked and crunched loudly. Alex was thankful when at last he found himself by the old shed. He made his way to the door, pushed it open and sneaked in. Inside, he flicked on a torch just as Cherry arrived.

'You didn't waste any time.'

'I found these in one of the drawers in our room,' said Cherry, and handed Alex a box of candles and some matches.

'Look at this place,' said Alex, flashing the torch around the shed. The walls were covered in shelves, filled with dust and pots of paint. Hanging on one wall were various garden implements. Alex quickly moved some old wooden boxes into a circle on the floor, with a larger box in the middle as a sort of table.

'Put the candles on that,' he said, and Cherry began lighting the candles, using melting wax to stick them to the box.

'This is cool!' said House as he came through the shed door.

'Freezing, more like,' said Inchy, arriving at the same time.

'I thought I said to count to ten before following each other,' complained Alex.

'I did. But House goes a lot slower than I do.'

Finally, Spit arrived.

'Cosy.'

Alex took the lead.

'Right, everyone, sit down. Inchy? Over to you.'

Everyone took their places round the box, now covered in burning candles. It looked like an enormous birthday cake.

'To be honest, I'd almost given up. Dante didn't go anywhere odd or do anything strange all week. It was like he was just a mental teacher who hated everyone, particularly Alex.'

Alex shrugged.

'Anyway, it was when I was following him at lunch today that it happened. You see, he usually spends lunch in his office. I've never managed to get in, but I've watched the door, so I know he just stays in there. But today he didn't; he went to the cellar.'

'What cellar?' asked Spit.

'It's under the hall. There's a door to it at the far end of that creepy corridor with all the old classrooms that nobody uses. I managed to sneak in after him and down the stairs. It's really scary down there. There isn't much light, but there's a load of old rooms, full of junk. I had to go really carefully so I didn't knock anything over. Then I heard voices up ahead. One of them was Dante's, but I didn't recognize the other one.'

'Did you see them?' asked House.

'Well, it was pretty nerve-racking, but I crept a bit closer. It was really, really hot and stuffy, and there was this strange red light. And then I saw them.'

'Dante?' asked Cherry.

'Yeah,' said Inchy. 'And someone else. I didn't see a face or anything, only a shadow on the wall, but it was someone bigger than Dante. Not just taller, but bigger in every way. This other person seemed to tower over him. And they were laughing. And then . . . I saw their shadows change.'

Inchy's face had turned white again, and his voice was shaking.

'What did you see?' asked Alex. 'You have to tell us.'

Inchy gulped.

'Wings,' he said. 'They *both* had wings.'

8
Busted

'I thought silver was werewolves,' said Cherry.

The gang had just left home and were on their way to school. It was already Friday again, the end of their third week on Earth and the day of the big football match.

'Isn't that vampires?' asked House.

'No,' said Inchy, 'vampires are crucifixes and holy water.'

'I thought holy water was zombies?' Alex put in.

'No,' corrected Cherry, 'nothing stops a zombie except lopping its head off.'

'A good punch in the face works,' said House. 'So long as the punch actually goes through its head and out the other side.'

'I didn't know that.'

'Well, now you do,' said House smugly.

'It's silver,' repeated Spit. 'Trust me – I've been researching it all last week and all this week. Demons is silver, I'm sure of it.'

After Inchy's revelation that there might be *two* demons at large in Green Hill School, the gang had doubled their efforts to prove it. Their schoolwork – even the footie match – had paled into insignificance against the possibility of being able to get back into Cloud Nine Academy not simply by serving out their punishment on Earth, but as heroes who'd foiled an evil demonic plot.

'What does silver do to them?' asked Cherry, as the gang turned on to Scholar's Walk, the road leading to the school. It was thronged with pupils. Alarmingly, most of them seemed to be wearing scarfs bearing the name of the team's opponents, The Black Crows.

'I don't really know,' said Spit, 'but everywhere I looked, it said that silver was useful against demons. Anything up to Level Five.'

'What's Level Five?' asked House.

Inchy stepped forward, his face serious.

'Level Fives are, like, the oldest of the old. They've been around since the beginning,' he explained. 'Hard as nails. They're rarely heard of now. They generally get lesser demons to do their dirty work. The only demon more powerful is the General, and we all know about him.'

'The General?'

'Satan,' said Cherry.

'Oh, right,' gulped House. 'That General. Oh dear.'

'So we don't actually know that it'll work, then?' said Alex.

'Look,' said Spit, 'there isn't a handy book in the human library called *Behold the Many Ways to Smite Demons!* None of us studied demons at Cloud Nine, and we can't just nip into the Heavenly Library, seeing as we're stuck on Earth. What else do you want me to do: go up and ask Dante if there's an easy way to kill him?'

Alex sighed with exasperation.

'Spit's done his best,' said Cherry. 'You shouldn't be so hard on him, Alex.'

'I'm not being hard on him. I'm not being hard on you, Spit. I just don't want us to mess this up.'

'Neither do I,' snapped Spit.

'So where are we going to get silver?' asked House.

'That's easy,' said Alex. 'The trophy cabinet at school. It's stuffed with silver cups and stuff. All we need to do is scrape some off and we're sorted.'

'We'll leave that to you, then,' said Inchy. 'It won't seem so out of the ordinary if you get caught.'

'When are you going to do it?' asked Cherry.

'In one of this morning's lessons,' said Alex. 'I'll ask to go to the toilet and sort it out then. Trust me.'

'I hate it when you say that,' said House.

Halfway through English, Alex asked to be excused. A couple of minutes later, though, he was nowhere near the toilets. Instead, he was gazing through the glass of the trophy cabinet.

First, Alex tried the door handle, but it was locked. With a quick look up and down the corridor, he pulled out his Lucky Dip and dug out some bits of tough wire. Bending the end of the wire, he inserted it into the lock, pushed, twisted and – bingo! – the lock popped open.

'Genius,' Alex muttered to himself.

Alex looked at the trophies. There were more than he realized, all different shapes and sizes. He pulled out some tissue paper from his pocket and rested it on the floor. Next he grabbed one of the really big trophies and, with the edge of a small penknife, he scraped some tiny shavings off the trophy and on to the tissue.

Five minutes later, he had a small pile of silver slivers. It didn't look like much, but Spit hadn't said how much silver was needed. Anyway, they weren't trying to kill Dante – just prove that he really was a demon. Besides, thought Alex, if he was out of lessons any longer, he might get caught. As he shut the cabinet, carefully folded up the tissue paper and headed back to English, Alex smiled to himself. If Dante *was* a demon, he had no idea what was about to hit him.

'Well? Did you get it?' asked Spit, as the gang sat outside, enjoying a few minutes of cool fresh air before geography. Around them, the noise of the playground filled the air. House came over to join them from where he'd been making friends with one of the lads from his chemistry lesson.

Alex nodded, patting his pocket.

Cherry was shaking her head.

'I don't like it. Dante might just be a human so horrible he's easily mistaken for a demon.'

'I know what I saw,' said Alex.

'Me too,' agreed House.

'And me,' added Inchy.

'But what all of you saw were wings,' mused Spit, 'and it's not just demons who have them, is it?'

'You're not suggesting Dante's an angel, are you?' asked Alex.

'I'm not suggesting anything. I'm just saying that we shouldn't jump to conclusions, that's all.'

'He's a demon, I know it,' said Alex. 'And we're going to get him.'

'Whatever. But don't say I didn't warn you.'

The school bell rang.

'Right,' said Alex, 'this is it.'

'What are you actually going to do?' asked Cherry.

Alex turned to Spit.

'Don't look at me,' said Spit, holding his hands up. 'I told you what I found out. There was nothing about how to actually *use* the silver once you've got it.'

Alex thought for a few seconds, then said, 'I've got a plan.'

'I hate it when you say that too,' sniffed House, and followed the rest of the gang into Dante's classroom.

The lesson began like most geography lessons – with Alex being hauled to the front of the room by Mr Dante for no apparent reason. But rather than trudging to the front as he did normally, Alex practically skipped up to Dante's desk.

'Yes, Mr Dante, sir?'

'Cloud,' sighed Dante theatrically, 'will there ever be a week, or even a day, that goes by without you irritating me?'

The rest of the class tittered, but Alex smiled up at the teacher, saying nothing.

'Cat got your tongue once again?'

Alex just grinned wider.

'So, the silent treatment. How very mature, Cloud.'

Without another word, Dante reached over to the desk, picked up the blackboard rubber and proceeded to paint Alex's face with chalk dust, just like he'd done before.

Which was when Alex put his plan into effect.

'Aaa . . .'

Alex fumbled in his pocket.

'Are you trying to say something, Cloud?' said Dante, leaning down towards him and cupping a hand to his twisted ear.

'AaaAAAA . . .'

Alex pulled out a carefully folded tissue.

'Speak up, Cloud,' snarled Dante, leaning closer still.

'Aaaa-AAAAA-AAAAACHOOO!'

Alex sneezed the contents of the tissue right into Dante's face.

It was a great plan. A foolproof plan. A work of genius!

For a moment Dante looked stunned. He stood there in front of the whole shocked class, swaying slightly. Alex stared at him, waiting for something hideous to happen. Perhaps it would be boils, or his skin would flake off? Perhaps his eyes would burst, or his head would explode? Whatever it was, it just *had* to be horrifically horrible and vile, surely!

Dante turned his head towards Alex and . . .

There was nothing wrong with him.

Or was there? There was something about his eyes, something about their colour . . . Something like flames dancing in them . . .

But before Alex could work out exactly what it was, Dante grabbed him by the scruff of the neck and frogmarched him out of the classroom, down the corridor and into his office.

'In there, Cloud!' he yelled, wiping his face with his jacket sleeve.

Alex found himself being thrown headlong into a musty-looking book cupboard. The door slammed and all light was extinguished to nothingness. The sound of the key turning behind him was followed by the noise of Dante's footsteps smartly departing his office and the door creaking shut. Then silence.

'That went well,' Alex muttered.

'There will be no more interruptions from Cloud for the rest of the day.' Dante glowered at the class.

'The rest of the day?' hissed Cherry to Inchy. 'But what about the match this afternoon?'

'You have something to say, Miss Cherry?' asked Dante, snapping round to stare at her.

Cherry looked at Dante. Was she imagining it,

or did the skin of his face seem red and sore, like he'd spent too long in the sun?

'Er, well,' began Cherry, 'it's just that we've got a footie match this afternoon and Alex is captain of our team. We need him.'

'Well, that *is* a shame,' said Dante, 'because he won't be seeing the light of day until four o'clock.'

'But that's not fair,' said House, opening his mouth and speaking before his brain had a chance to close it.

'Cloud has only himself to blame; such disgusting behaviour must be punished. Would you like to join him?'

House gulped and shook his head.

'No, I thought not,' smiled Dante. 'Any of the rest of Cloud's friends? I'm more than happy to shut you all away, you know. From what I've seen of your team practices, it's the only way you'll be spared the embarrassment of defeat this afternoon.'

The gang looked at each other, desperation in their eyes. But there was nothing they could do.

'Good,' said Dante, then turned to the rickety old blackboard and scratched on to its surface the rest of the lesson and rather a lot of homework.

Back in the cupboard, Alex was exploring. It was hot and utterly dark, but by feeling with his hands, he had already discovered that the cupboard was much bigger than he'd realized.

If only I'd brought a torch, he thought, taking another step forward, his hands groping in the blackness. At last, Alex's fingers brushed against a switch, flooding the cupboard with light.

A rattling, bony hand landed on his shoulder with a loud *crack*.

Alex screamed, but no one heard him.

No one at all.

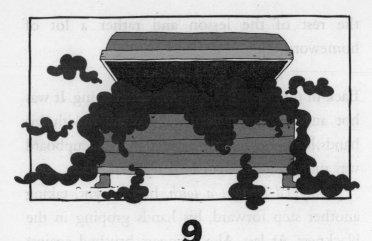

9
Skeletons in the Closet

'Why do boys' changing rooms always smell so awful?' asked Cherry, sneaking in from the girls' changing rooms across the hall.

'Apparently,' said Inchy, 'it's the smell of animal ferocity, of determination, of that lust for the winning goal, of –'

'Wet socks and boredom,' cut in House. 'I hate waiting for the match to start. I get nervous.'

Inchy took a step away from his big friend. He knew very well that when House got nervous, his clumsiness got worse. He looked up at the clock.

'Well, there's only five minutes left. Just enough

time for us to get indigestion from lunch.'

'That wasn't a lunch,' muttered House, collapsing on to a bench, which groaned ominously. 'That was death by mashed potato. I can hardly move.'

'We might be in with a chance, then,' sneered Spit. 'If we stick you in front of the goal, you'll block the whole thing.'

House didn't respond. His mind was still coming to terms with the fact they were really about to play their first five-a-side football match on Earth. With only four players.

'I hope Alex is OK,' said Cherry, almost as if she'd read his thoughts.

'Dante might let him out,' chirped House hopefully. 'He can't keep him locked up all day, can he?' He tugged at his armband. 'Then I wouldn't have to be captain. That makes me nervous too.'

'This is Dante we're talking about,' replied Inchy, moving even further away. 'He's not exactly renowned for fair play, is he?'

Spit stood up and kicked a lump of muddy grass across the concrete floor.

'There's no way we're going to win,' he muttered dejectedly. 'We might as well not even bother turning up – we're going to get killed out there.'

'What choice do we have?' said Cherry, running her fingers through her bright red hair. 'We've just got to go out and do our best. It's only a game.'

'But it's not only a game, is it?' said Spit. 'It's just another way for us to be made to look like idiots. Life must be much easier for Dante – messing up other people's lives rather than having yours messed up for you.'

The rest of the team turned to look at Spit incredulously.

'You'd rather be like Dante, then?' asked Cherry. 'Is that what you're saying?'

'I'm not saying anything,' said Spit, scuffing his football boots on the floor, 'but it's pretty obvious that if Dante likes you, life's much easier.'

'Well, why don't you go and get all chummy with him, then?' challenged House, his temper flaring. 'Go on! Go and be his mate instead. Join the Other Side, why don't you?'

Spit didn't reply. He just turned and walked off through the door that led to the pitch.

'As team talks go,' said Inchy, 'that wasn't one of the greatest.'

'I'm sorry, but why can't he just be like the

rest of us, instead of all awkward and moody?'

'Spit's just Spit,' said Cherry. 'He's not bad really.'

'I know,' admitted House gloomily. 'I'm just worried. I'm really not cut out for captain.'

'It's funny,' mused Cherry. 'Alex may get us into all sorts of scrapes, but we do need him.'

'Come on,' encouraged Inchy, 'we might as well follow Spit. There's no point trying to pretend we don't have to play.'

'Spit!' yelled Cherry. 'Wait!'

Spit turned as the rest of their depleted team met him on the touchline. It looked like half the school had turned out to witness the gang's humiliation.

'We do this together, yeah?' said Cherry. 'As a team. Like Alex said.'

Spit nodded.

'And you're right, Cherry,' said House. 'It is just a game.' He forced a smile. 'Come on,' he said, slapping Inchy hard on the back and sending the smaller angel flying. 'Let's give them our worst.'

'That shouldn't be too difficult,' muttered Spit.

The team had hardly had a chance to start warming up when they first noticed something odd was happening. First the wind dropped, then the birds stopped singing. Finally, a huge dark cloud drifted across the sun, plunging the pitch into gloom. Even the crowds of chattering kids on the sidelines fell silent.

'What's going on?' asked House.

In reply, Inchy just pointed.

'It can't be,' hissed Spit.

'It is,' said Cherry.

Their opponents, The Black Crows, each looking about two metres tall in their all-black kit, had emerged from the changing rooms and were making their way on to the pitch. Jogging in front of them, wearing a worn tracksuit and a nasty grin, was the referee.

Mr Dante.

Alex screamed until his voice caught in his throat like a snared rat. His heart felt like it was doing its best to thump its way out of his chest. The hand on his shoulder hadn't moved – it just stayed there, firm and cold. Rooted to the spot, Alex could only close his eyes and wait for something horrible to happen – for the owner of the hand to reveal him- or herself as a flesh-eating zombie. Or a terrifying monster ready to chew out his guts.

But nothing happened. Nothing at all. Tentatively opening one eye, Alex turned to look at the hand.

And screamed again.

The hand was made of hard white bones, shining in the harsh light of the single naked bulb. Above the hand hung a skeleton, a huge hook stuck painfully through its ribs.

Frantically, Alex batted the hand off his shoulder. It fell away with a soft plastic clatter. And suddenly he realized that it was just a model – the sort of thing human teachers used in lessons.

Alex let out a long breath. Now that he didn't have to worry about having his guts sucked out, he felt much calmer. And it seemed that, apart from the skeleton, the cupboard didn't contain anything out of the ordinary. In fact, the cupboard's contents were *entirely* ordinary: boxes, folders, a couple of battered old leather suitcases, two coats, an umbrella and a hat – nothing like the kind of stuff Alex would have expected a demon to own. He was rather disappointed.

'What's the point of being a demon if you don't have at least *some* weird and creepy stuff hanging around?'

For the first time, Alex felt a twinge of doubt. Was it possible that he and House had imagined what had happened in Dante's office? Had Inchy really seen wings in the cellar?

Well, if Dante was a demon, then there was certainly no incriminating evidence in the cupboard, that was for sure. Time to look elsewhere.

Alex tried the door. It was definitely locked, but it did feel a bit flimsy. An expert at getting out of tight squeezes, Alex reckoned he might just be able to force it open. Bracing himself against the back wall of the cupboard, he placed both feet on the door and pushed hard.

The door didn't budge a centimetre.

Instead, the wall behind Alex fell away and he tumbled backwards, coming to rest on a stone floor in a room with no windows.

The room was lit by four enormous red candles clasped in a huge metal claw nailed to the far wall. In the centre of the floor was a wooden trunk. The walls of the room were decorated with curious signs scratched into the surface. It wasn't exactly the kind of place a normal geography teacher would have behind his office cupboard. And it certainly wasn't somewhere Alex wanted to be.

Alex's mind was racing now, chasing itself down a nightmare path.

'Stay calm,' he muttered to himself. 'Stay calm.'

Alex looked at the candles in the far wall with a shiver. He wanted to leave as fast as he could, but something was making him stay: a sense that he was about to find something that the rest of the gang couldn't just ignore. Hard proof that Dante was a demon.

Under the candles stood a strange chair. Pulling himself to his feet, Alex edged over, wanting to see it up close, but at the same time terrified of getting any nearer. He reached out his hand to touch the seat, which was smooth and cool, but it was the arms that drew his eye; they were covered in razor-sharp shards, a riot of edges and points that made the chair look like a frozen explosion of jagged grey metal. It was as if to sit on the chair properly you had to be willing to cut yourself to shreds.

Not keen to try out the chair for size, but unwilling to take his eyes off it, Alex backed over to the trunk. No clasp held it shut and, without thinking, he heaved it open. The lid was heavy, and as he pulled it back, Alex felt the strangest of sensations, almost as if he were opening the lid of a tomb.

The inside of the trunk was so thick with darkness it was like it was filled with treacle, its shadows seeming to spill out into the room. But eventually Alex's eyes were able to make out some shapes. He lowered his head to get a better look, tentatively reaching inside.

'Ouch!'

Alex yanked his hand out of the trunk.

A cut, deep and red, lay across the top of his thumb. Gazing back into the trunk, Alex's eyes could just make out the shape of a dagger. More carefully this time, he reached in and tugged it free.

Alex stared at the knife in horror; a thin groove ran down its whole length from the very tip of the blade to the end of the bone handle. The blade was dull, something dried on its surface. Alex didn't even have to guess; he knew it was blood.

Shaking now, but unable to stop himself, Alex looked again into the trunk. Something else was there — a dark rectangular shadow. With both hands, he reached in and pulled out a black leather book. It was heavy and, as Alex opened it, a chill ran through him. The pages were engraved with a strange language, and something told him that this thing, this collection of pages and words, was something he should never have seen. It was a creeping terror now that held him and, as he placed the book to one side, it was all Alex could do to force himself to take just one more look.

Pressed into a corner, almost as if it were cowering at the very bottom of the trunk, was a small, black box.

Alex knew that he should run; slam the trunk shut, bolt from the room and leave the school forever. But this simple box called to him in a voice he couldn't quite hear, but had to obey.

The box was smooth and cold, like glass and ice combined, but it opened easily – almost too easily. Alex gazed in.

It was like looking through a window into space. The inside of the box was dark and seemed to be much bigger than the outside, but right in its heart a bright shape was moving and swaying, gently pulsating like a blob of wax in a lava lamp. For a moment, it was strangely beautiful. Then Alex saw *why* the vivid blue shape was moving – it was trying to escape. It wasn't swaying gently, it was writhing and twisting, as if it had sensed that the lid was open and was trying to get out of the box and as far away from it as possible. But all around the intense blue form were woven ropes of shadow, and the dark chains held it fast.

And as he watched the shape desperately struggling to get free from its prison, Alex suddenly realized what he was holding.

The football match was going very, very badly.

'What are you doing, Spit?' screamed Cherry, running back into their own half. 'Do you want us to lose or what?'

'What did you want me to do?' he yelled back. 'It was three on one!'

'But you didn't even *try* to tackle them!'

'Oh, so it's all my fault we're losing, is it?'

Cherry didn't even bother to answer.

House and Inchy looked on from the goal. Inchy's face was well spattered with mud. House, however, was completely covered. The one part of him that was clear of the gooey sludge was his eyes, but only because he'd just wiped them.

'We need Alex,' said House.

'No, we need a miracle,' replied Inchy.

'But playing one man down is just totally unfair.'

'It's what Dante's best at, I reckon.'

Dante's voice echoed across the pitch: 'Foul! Free kick!'

Cheers rang out from the sidelines. It was a horrible sound. Back at Cloud Nine, everyone used to cheer for their team, The Wingers, but here it seemed like they were the least popular team ever.

'Foul? What foul?' asked House, turning. 'We weren't even playing!'

Dante strode towards them.

'You!' he yelled, pointing at one of the other team.

A large gorilla-like boy lolloped towards them.

'Take the free kick here,' Dante commanded, handing the ball to the boy.

'But there wasn't a —'

Before House had a chance to finish, the boy passed the ball towards one of his team-mates. Cherry sprinted to intercept, but another of their opponents stuck out a leg, tripping her up.

'Foul!' she screamed. 'That was a foul!'

'Play on,' said Dante.

'No diving!' shrieked one of the tall girls who had insulted Cherry on the gang's first day at school. 'Get up, chubby!'

Thundering towards the angels' goal, one of the Crows niftily nutmegged House and smashed the ball past Inchy into the back of the net.

'Great goal, Jackson!' bellowed Dante, blowing his whistle sharply. 'That's full time! The Black Crows win, six–two!'

The crowd went wild. Whooping, the Crows rushed off towards the changing rooms, exchanging high-fives. Dante strode after them, ignoring Cherry, who was still sprawled in the mud, nursing her ankle.

Spit jogged over and held out his hand.

'I'm fine,' said Cherry, pushing him away, 'I'm fine.'

House and Inchy joined them.

'I think we've lost,' said Inchy.

'We lost even before we came on the pitch,' said Spit.

'Well, it's not like you did anything to help, is it?' hissed Cherry. 'You might as well have been on their side – you played like a total muppet.'

Spit opened his mouth to reply, but was interrupted.

'Look!' cried House, pointing towards the school.

The gang turned to see a figure charging across the grass towards them.

'It's Alex,' said Inchy. 'I don't think I've ever seen him run so fast. What do you think he's done now? Blown up the headmaster's office?'

Alex skidded across the grass and landed in a pile at their feet. A few of the kids still hanging around on the touchline hooted with laughter.

'What's up?' asked Cherry. 'You look like you've seen a ghost.'

'We lost, by the way,' said Spit.

'It doesn't matter,' puffed Alex. 'Not now. Not after what I found.'

'Dante's a demon, then?' asked Inchy.

'Worse,' said Alex. 'A lot, lot worse. He locked me in a cupboard with this secret room behind it. There was this freaky chair, and four candles –'

'Was the chair covered in lots of sharp, spiky stuff, like it was supposed to cut you?' asked Spit.

Alex nodded.

'I've read about them. It's a Weeping Chair.'

'What's a Weeping Chair?' asked Cherry, although she suspected she didn't want to hear the answer.

'Demons use them to contact each other. The demon has to sit on their chair so that the sharp bits cut into them – their blood acts like a phone line. The chair weeps their blood, so it's called a Weeping Chair.'

'That's sick,' said Inchy.

'That's demons,' replied Spit. 'And the four candles above the chair tell us exactly what sort we're dealing with – a Level Four Fire Demon.'

'We're dead,' whispered House. 'We are so dead.'

'What else did you find, Alex?' asked Cherry.

The blond angel was silent for a moment. He tried to speak, but his voice was stuck in his throat.

'What was it?' asked Spit. 'What did you see?'

'A soul,' said Alex finally, his voice cracking. 'I found a trapped soul.'

10
Council of War

Midnight, and the whole gang was back in the shed at the bottom of the garden, huddled up in their warmest clothes to keep out the cool night air. Despite their disagreements on the football pitch, they each knew that what Alex had discovered was much more important. Dante was a demon. Unquestionably. Now they had to work together to figure out what to do about it. Silently, they racked their brains for any hint of an idea that might help them. Seconds stretched into minutes. Finally, a voice pierced the silence.

'Who's got the biscuits?'

'You what?' said Cherry disbelievingly.

'Biscuits,' repeated Big House. 'I'm hungry.'

'How can you think about your stomach at a time like this?' asked Inchy.

'It's difficult to miss, really, isn't it?' grinned Spit, poking House in the tummy.

'Well, we can't work out how to save the world from an insane demon on empty stomachs, can we?'

Alex smiled and held out a plastic bag.

'Here you go, mate.'

House took the bag and moments later was passing around not only biscuits, but crisps and cans of lemonade.

'Right,' said Alex with a deep breath. 'It's time to take Dante down.'

'What, just like that?' grumbled Spit. 'Five not-quite angels against a Level Four Fire Demon?'

He laughed coldly, shaking his head.

'What is your problem?' asked House, finishing his third packet of crisps. 'Scared?'

Spit turned to face him.

'Of a Level Four Demon? You bet I'm scared. Only an idiot wouldn't be. Which explains why you're not.'

'Taking on a Level Four does sound insane,'

admitted Inchy, 'but what choice do we have?'

'Quite an obvious one, really,' said Spit. 'We don't do anything.'

'Are you ill?' asked Cherry.

Spit ignored her.

'And what about what Alex saw?' spluttered House. 'What kind of monster keeps a chair made of razor blades and a soul trapped in a box? We can't just ignore that – we've got to do something!'

'This isn't some fun adventure, you idiot, this is serious! If Dante's a Level Four, then we're dead! Don't you get it? *Finito!* Game over!'

'Shouting at House isn't going to help, is it?' interrupted Cherry. 'So why don't you do something more useful, like shutting up?'

The conversation exploded.

'Oh, so you think you can take on a Level Four, do you?'

'Well, at least I'd try!'

'What good's trying if you end up dead?'

'Go boil your head!'

'Only if you fry yours first!'

Alex watched his friends screaming at each other and knew it was time to play his trump card.

A heavy thud silenced the argument. Four pairs

of eyes turned to stare at what was now sitting on the box in the middle of the shed. Alex folded his arms and waited.

'What's that?' asked Cherry.

'It can't be,' said Inchy.

'It is.'

House took a step forward.

'It's a book,' he said.

'Not just any book,' said Spit, looking straight at Alex. 'Why didn't you say you had this?'

'You didn't give me a chance,' Alex replied. 'Besides, you'd probably have started shouting at me about what an idiot I was to nick it.'

'You've got a point,' said Inchy, 'although perhaps *suicidal* idiot would be more accurate.'

'But it's just a book,' said Cherry. 'What's the big deal?'

His pale face whiter than ever, Spit gingerly reached out his hand, almost as though he was afraid the book was red hot.

'If Dante finds out you've got this . . .'

'*When* Dante finds out we've got this,' corrected Inchy, shaking his head, 'he's going to know we're on to him.'

'He might not notice for ages,' protested Alex. 'I closed the secret door on my way out. He knows I picked the lock of the cupboard to get away, so I'm going to be in big trouble on Monday, but that doesn't mean he knows I found the hidden room.'

'And it's only a book, anyway,' repeated House. 'Just a big book with a black cover and no title. What are you worrying about?'

'Watch,' said Alex, and he picked up a candle and touched the flame to the book.

A flash seared through the shed, making everyone gasp. For a few moments, no one could see. Then, as the glare faded, each of them stared at the book.

Etched into the black cover sat the number *666* – and from each figure, flames licked high into the air.

'You have *got* to be joking,' breathed Cherry.

'I don't hear anyone laughing,' said Inchy.

Alex looked at Spit, who threw up his hands. 'Well, everyone, we are now the proud, soon-to-be-dead owners of a *Necronomicon*.'

'Necro what?' asked House.

'*Necronomicon*. Otherwise known as *The Book of the Dead*,' said Inchy, leafing through his mental library. 'It's written by people who are dead to everything except darkness. It's full of terrible dark rites and rituals, instructions for making monsters, zombies and other icky stuff.'

House looked horrified.

'And I thought the worst book I'd ever come across was *Intermediate Maths*.'

The discussion of 'What To Do About Dante' went round and round in circles and long into the night. Inchy suggested hacking into the school computer system to see if they could discover what he was up to by following him on CCTV. House's idea was more simple. It involved creeping up behind Dante, hitting him on the head with a big piece of wood, then dragging him before the Council of Heaven. Eventually it was Cherry who came up with the only plan that actually made any sense at all.

'It's the best way,' she said, looking at the rest of the gang. 'We already know what's behind the cupboard in Dante's office, thanks to Alex. And we now know that Dante's a demon. What we don't know is why Demon Dante was in the cellar – or who he was with. Maybe if we find that out, we'll know exactly what he's up to. Then we can do something about it.'

'So what do you suggest?' asked Spit.

'We go back to the cellar. That's where the answer is.'

'I'm not sure,' said Inchy, sounding nervous. 'Couldn't we just give hacking into the computers a go?'

'I'm with Cherry on this,' said Alex. 'We need to know if Dante is planning something. It could be putting the whole school in danger. And the best lead we've got is what you saw in the cellar, Inchy.'

'I know. That's what scares me.'

Alex stood up.

'It's too risky to try it while we're at school. Too many people around – and Dante might drop in as well. We'll sneak in there tomorrow night when the place is empty, suss out the cellar, then sneak away again. No one will ever know we were there.'

Spit grimaced.

'You make it sound so easy.'

'It's a gift,' grinned Alex. 'Anyone got any better ideas?'

He was answered with silence.

'That's it, then. Tomorrow night it is.'

11
Into the Dark

It was just past midnight and the gang were huddled against the playground wall. Getting past Tabbris had been more tricky than they had anticipated – the old Guardian Angel might have retired from Special Operations, but his instincts were still surprisingly sharp. He had nearly caught them as they sneaked down the hall, almost as if he could sense that something was wrong.

Luckily, the gang were able to duck into the shadows and crouch, holding their breath, until Tabbris limped back into the living room, where he was listening to one of his old vinyl gramophone records of marching music.

Finally, they had managed to sneak through the front door, leaving it on the latch. Now all they had to do was get into the school.

'So how do we get in? I *do* hope we haven't come all this way only to discover that we're shut out.'

The tone of Spit's voice suggested he hoped exactly the opposite.

'I left one of the windows open in the toilets.'

'But the caretaker might've locked it again?' asked Cherry hopefully.

'Well,' said Alex, a grin sneaking across his face, 'I say "left it open", but I guess a more accurate description would be that I sort of broke the lock.'

'That's vandalism,' said Inchy.

'That's forward thinking. Come on; this way.'

Before anyone had a chance to reply, Alex scampered off towards the school building.

A couple of minutes later, the gang were in a corner of the playground, underneath the window to the boys' toilet. Shadows were playing chase on the walls as dark smoky clouds drifted silently across a crescent moon. A faint breeze danced in the air, kicking up bits of litter and rustling branches, carrying with it strange sounds from far off.

'Can't say I like this,' said Inchy.

'What's not to like?' replied Spit with a curl of his lip. 'The dark? The cold? The fact that we're about to break into school in the middle of the night to try and discover what a Level Four Demon is playing at in the cellar? You mean this isn't your idea of fun?'

Inchy didn't bother to reply.

'Smells a bit,' observed Cherry, sniffing. 'You sure there isn't another way in?'

'Not that I know of,' said Alex. Tapping House on the shoulder, he added, 'Give us a leg-up.'

House leaned forward, grabbed Alex's foot and launched him up the wall. With a smack, Alex's head cracked on the stone window ledge.

'Sorry.'

'A bit less of a leg-up,' winced Alex, rubbing his head.

More carefully this time, House boosted Alex up to the window above. With a push, it swung open and Alex wriggled in.

'Who's next?' asked House, rubbing his hands together.

The others glanced at each other nervously.

'Ladies first,' said Spit.

Cherry, then Inchy and finally Spit all followed Alex in through the window. Last, but by no means least, House leapt up, grabbed the window frame and hauled himself on to the window ledge. Textbook stuff. He was pretty proud of the way he'd remembered everything he'd read about scaling walls in his Guardian Angel manual.

What he wasn't so proud of was the way he then jumped inside, only to land with his left foot in a toilet.

'Classy,' said Spit. 'Smooth, professional – talented even. I'd probably give you, ooh, eight out of ten for technique and two out of ten for artistic impression.'

One look from House was enough to wipe the smirk off Spit's face as he shook his foot free, dripping water across the floor.

Alex was already by the toilet door, his torch spreading a path of light down the hallway outside.

'Ready?'

Before anyone could back out, Alex was off. The rest of the gang followed, House squelching behind them.

'Can you hear that rattling?' whispered Inchy.

Beside him Cherry strained to listen.

'There's nothing there. I can't hear a thing.'

'You must be able to,' replied Inchy. 'It's a sort of scratching . . .'

'What, like the sound of demon claws dragging along the floor?' suggested Spit.

'I'm serious,' said Inchy. 'There's something over there, I'm sure of it.'

The gang had been trying to ignore the strange sounds the school was making in the dark. Inchy wasn't exactly helping.

'Will you shut up?' hissed Cherry. 'It's creepy enough without you hearing things!'

'And why's it so warm?' asked House, his forehead beaded with sweat.

'The heating must still be on,' said Alex, leading the gang ever closer to the cellar.

'That doesn't make sense. Why would the heating be on at night?'

'How should I know?' said Alex. 'But it is; this radiator's boiling.'

A rattle echoed down the hall.

'See?' said Inchy. 'That's the rattle I was talking about! It's the pipes.'

'How about we shove you in to find out what

it is, then?' said Spit with an evil grin.

'Erm, I wouldn't fit,' said Inchy, backing away nervously.

'Are you sure about that?'

Inchy thought better of making a smart reply.

'Probably just rats. That'll be it . . .' His voice trailed off. 'We're here!'

Everyone peered forward and, sure enough, just ahead lay a small door. It didn't look much like the kind of door behind which a demon would hide. But then again, Dante's cupboard had seemed innocent enough at first.

Inchy reached out, turned the door handle and pushed. Without a sound, the door swung open, as if inviting them into the darkness beyond.

The gang walked in single file down a narrow stair, each step taking them further and further into the unknown. And the further they went, the warmer it became.

'Do you have to walk so close to me?' hissed Cherry.

'Do you have to walk so slowly?' replied House.

'I'm not walking slowly, I'm just being careful.'

House didn't reply. Instead, he lost his footing

on the edge of the next step and slipped, taking Cherry with him.

Then Alex.

And finally – with a yelp – Inchy.

'Well, it's a good job we're all being so quiet,' said Spit, standing at the rear. 'Otherwise Dante might hear us coming.'

The gang turned as one to look daggers at him.

'Dante's not here,' said Alex, scrambling to his feet.

'You know that for sure?' asked Cherry.

'Of course I do. He'll be at home watching the telly or something.'

Alex didn't sound very convincing, even to himself.

At last the gang were back on their feet and edging forward until they came to the end of the stairs and into a short corridor that ended in a rusty iron door.

'Through there. I didn't go very far last time, but it's through that door.'

The fear in Inchy's voice was more than a little obvious.

Before they moved any further, Alex turned to face his friends.

'We have to agree something before we go on.'

'What's that?' asked Spit. 'Not to smack you in the face when this all goes horribly wrong?'

Cherry punched Spit in the leg.

'Ow!'

'We have to agree that, no matter what happens, we're all in this together, OK?' Alex looked at the team.

Almost everyone nodded.

'We may fall out now and again, but we're friends, and the only way we can get through this – the only way we can beat Dante – is by sticking together.'

'Nice speech,' said Spit. 'Now can we get this over with?'

As they edged forward, the air became heavy. Beyond the iron door, a warren of rooms was lit by a strange red glow that seemed to be coming from somewhere off in the distance. Several of the rooms had strange scratch marks on the walls, similar to the ones in Dante's secret room upstairs. Alex led the gang on, always trying to head towards the red light, but it never seemed to get any closer.

'Maybe we should turn back before we get lost?' suggested Cherry.

'We can't,' said Alex. 'We haven't found anything yet.'

'Got any string?' asked House. 'We could tie one end here and then unwind it as we go, so that we know which way to come back.'

'You know,' said Spit, patting his pockets, 'this is the first day I've ever come out without at least one ball of string. What are the odds, eh?'

Alex let out a muffled curse. 'And I forgot the Lucky Dip.'

'How can it get this hot?' muttered Cherry, wiping sweat from her eyes.

'We're underground,' said Inchy, 'so the earth around us is acting like insulation. The heat's got nowhere to escape to, so it just keeps getting hotter and hotter.'

'Are you really clever, or are you just good at making stuff up?' asked Spit.

'But why?' asked Cherry, ignoring Spit. 'I mean, this is just a cellar. What's the point of keeping it hot?'

With a clatter, House pitched forward against a door and crashed through it into the next room.

'Sorry,' said House from the floor. 'Tripped over.'

'But there was nothing to trip over,' replied Inchy.

'You're forgetting his own feet,' said Spit.

The gang edged over towards where House had disappeared.

'It's cooler in here. There's a draught,' said Cherry.

'Let's just stick to the plan and follow the red light,' suggested Alex. 'I've got a feeling that's where we'll find out what's going on down here.'

The gang crept on. After what felt like an age, the red light seemed to be getting close. Finally, the maze of rooms opened out into a larger cellar. The light was stronger still – it seemed to lick up and down the walls.

'Well, if you're from Hell,' observed Inchy, 'I guess this is a home from home.'

'It's even hotter in here,' panted Cherry, trying to catch her breath. 'I'm not sure how long I can stand it. What on Earth is making it so warm?'

'That is,' said House.

An enormous beast sat glaring at them from the far end of the cavern. Its face was a mass of glowing eyes. Explosive tongues of flame shot out from a growling mouth of black teeth. And from its body stretched numerous spider-like legs, reaching round the walls.

'We're dead,' said Spit, backing away.

The flames licked forward across the floor of the cavern, seeming to taste their way towards the gang.

'Let's get out of here,' Cherry whimpered, her eyes wide.

'I'm with you on that,' said Alex. 'Being eaten by a Fire Demon wasn't part of my plan.'

Slowly, the gang started to back away.

All except Inchy.

'What are you doing?' hissed Alex. 'Move!'

But Inchy didn't move.

'Come on!' cried Cherry, panic edging into her voice.

Inchy turned to the gang.

'It's not a demon,' he shouted. 'Look at it!'

The gang all stared at the hideous thing.

'It's a furnace,' said Inchy, his voice quieter. 'That's all it is; an old-fashioned furnace.'

And sure enough, now they looked closer, the angels could see that the bulky beast wasn't alive at all. It was made of metal. Sooty rusty metal. Its 'legs' were just a collection of pipes that ran off in all directions. The black teeth that had seemed so terrifying were just the bars of a grate. It was the flickering red glare of the cellar that had made it seem alive.

'It doesn't make much sense, though.'

'What doesn't?'

'Well, look at it,' said Inchy. 'That's a coal furnace. It's ancient! It must have been here since the school was first built. But the heating must be run on oil or electricity now.'

Alex shrugged, looking around the cellar.

'But what's *really* weird is the fact that it's going full blast in the middle of the night. For it to be this hot, someone should be down here stuffing coal into it non-stop. But there's no one here. *No one!*'

'What are you saying?' asked Cherry.

'I'm not saying anything,' Alex replied. 'All I know is that a furnace can't keep going all by itself.'

'Something else is weird too,' chipped in House. 'That strange green blob on top of it.'

Everyone gazed at where House was pointing.

'It looks like a rugby ball,' said Cherry.

'And you've seen a lot of rugby balls that glow green, have you?'

Inchy edged forward, his eyes fixed on the strange object.

'Be careful,' shouted Alex. 'That furnace looks like it might explode at any moment.'

But Inchy wasn't listening. He was getting close to the furnace. Too close – he could smell something burning now. But he could almost see what the strange object was . . .

'Inchy! Come back!' called Cherry. 'What is he doing?'

The tiny angel had edged almost right up to the roaring furnace, peering towards the glowing green ball. Suddenly, without warning, he leapt upright as if he'd been stung and hared back to the others.

'It's not a rugby ball,' he puffed, skidding to a halt, his face red with the heat and his hair and clothes smouldering slightly. 'And I'd like to suggest we run away right now and as far as possible.'

'Why?' asked Alex. 'What's up? What's wrong? What is it?'

'It's a demon egg.'

12
Cat and Mouse

'Whoa!' Alex whistled. 'A demon egg. Looks like Dante's going to be a daddy!'

'Can you stop cracking jokes for ten seconds,' snarled Spit, 'and listen to Inchy – let's get as far away from it as possible!'

'What, and just leave it here and pretend we never saw it? We can't walk around school knowing there's a demon egg under our feet and not do anything about it!'

'I can,' said Spit.

'Me too,' agreed Inchy.

Alex turned.

'Spit's got a point,' shrugged Cherry. 'This has got too big for us. We have to get help. Let's tell Gabriel.'

Alex couldn't believe what he was hearing.

'Are you serious?' he snapped. 'This just makes it even more likely that he'd hog all the glory for himself. Remember the plan? We're going to sort this out ourselves and go back to Heaven as heroes. Besides, why should Gabriel believe anything we say? We're down here on Earth because he thinks we're troublemakers. If we turn up with some story about a Level Four Demon and a big green egg, do you really think he'll believe us? Well, do you?'

Alex could feel anger rising in him. It was a feeling he didn't like. There was something about it, a mixture of excitement and adrenaline, but also a sense that he was losing control. And angels weren't supposed to lose control. They'd definitely been on Earth for far too long. It was time to go.

For a few seconds the gang faced each other in utter silence. The air hummed and throbbed as the furnace continued to pump out heat into its rattling tentacle-like pipes. The shadows around them seemed to grow thicker, pressing in on them, almost as if they were trying to listen.

House cracked his knuckles.

'Let's smash it.'

Everyone turned.

'I mean it. Let's smash it. That way, whatever Dante is planning is ruined, we've won, and Gabriel will have to let us back into Heaven. Simple.'

He took a step towards the furnace and the egg.

'Just so you know, House,' interrupted Inchy, '*before* you try to smash it: demon eggs aren't like normal eggs. You can't break them and dip bits of toast in. Not only are the shells really hard, they're filled with acid strong enough to melt through absolutely anything.'

'So not a good idea, then?'

Inchy shook his head.

'We could steal it,' suggested Alex, 'and take it to Tabbris. He'll contact Gabriel and before we know it, we'll be back at Cloud Nine and up to our old tricks!'

'And when Dante turns up in a few hours to check on his precious egg,' said Spit, 'what do you think will happen then?'

'Dante wouldn't stand a chance. Tabbris was

in Special Operations – he's got the Order of Raphael, for Heaven's sake. He'd wipe the floor with him.'

'Why are you always so confident?' asked Cherry. 'Tabbris is *old* – he's retired, isn't he? He can't be as tough as he used to be. We got past him tonight, didn't we? And anyway, who's to say that Dante hasn't got the egg rigged with some kind of alarm system?'

'An egg alarm?' exclaimed Alex. 'Are you serious?'

'Let's just leave it where it is.'

The gang stared at Spit.

'Well, it's not like anyone's come up with a decent alternative, is it? I say leave it. It's the safest plan.'

Alex felt his blood rising. Bubbling up inside him like milk boiling over in a microwave. He wanted to grab Spit and –

'Ssssh!'

Cherry hissed out the warning.

'I heard something.'

The gang fell quiet. For a long moment, silence reigned. Then they all heard it – the terrifying sound of firm, measured footsteps, each one louder and closer than the last.

'There's someone down here,' moaned House.

'We're trapped,' said Cherry. 'We can't go back the way we came. What if we bump into whoever's coming?'

'Stay calm. This place is like a labyrinth. We'll have to leave the egg and find another way out,' Alex muttered through clenched teeth. 'Come on!'

Ducking through a low doorway, they left the big cellar, the red light of the furnace fading behind them. Soon the gang were tiptoeing through what seemed like pitch blackness, hands stretched out in the dark.

'That's me,' hissed Inchy.

'No, it's me,' squealed Cherry indignantly.

'Sorry,' muttered House.

'Do that again and you will be,' said Spit.

'Quiet!' shushed Alex. 'The footsteps are getting close!'

Silence fell over them like a thick blanket. The angels hardly dared to breathe. There was no sound anywhere. Except for the footsteps. Coming closer, closer. Until they were right outside the room the gang were hiding in.

And then they stopped.

It was all Alex could do to stop himself

screaming. He could hear the sound of ragged breathing now. It sounded so close, almost close enough to –

Warm air brushed through his hair.

'Someone's here,' oozed a voice they all recognized. It was Dante. 'Yes, I know you're down here. What are you doing, I wonder? And where are you, hmm?'

Alex froze as a darker shadow appeared in the doorway, its slick blackness edging towards him. He could barely breathe. He wanted to run, but he couldn't move.

The voice came again.

'Is that you, Cloud?'

Alex's heart stopped.

'Are you the one who's stolen my book? Are you down here now? Oh, that would be delicious . . .'

For a moment, the shadow paused in the doorway and every one of the angels held their breath. Then, unbearably slowly, it turned away. The sound of footsteps echoed out again, slowly fading away as Mr Dante headed towards the furnace room.

For a few moments the gang stood like statues, unmoving.

Then Big House leaned over to Alex.

'Dante knows you're here.'

'Not yet he doesn't,' Alex whispered back. 'He's just guessing. He didn't see any of us.'

'But he knows *somebody*'s here,' breathed Spit.

'We've got to get out,' said Cherry. 'Now.'

'But how?'

'Wait a minute,' said House, raising his hand. 'Can you feel the draught? We're back in that room I found earlier!'

'You didn't find it,' said Spit. 'You fell into it.'

'Same difference. There's still a draught – and a draught has to come from somewhere, right? It might be a way out.'

'OK,' replied Alex decisively. 'House, you lead. Follow that draught.'

The gang filed off, trying to muffle the sound of their footsteps. It was a terrifying journey through room after room. As their eyes adjusted to the darkness, strange shapes seemed to loom out of the shadows to block their way – only to be revealed as stacks of old chairs, or piles of rubbish. Finally, after what seemed like an age, a faint glimmer appeared in front of them. Moonlight!

'Almost there,' whispered Alex. 'House, whatever you do, don't –'

House walked straight into a pile of cardboard boxes. With a thunderous crash of breaking glass, old test tubes and beakers went flying in all directions.

For a moment, there was silence. Then, from somewhere behind them came the sound of footsteps again. But this time they were running.

'Move!'

The gang bolted.

'Don't push!' yelled Inchy, as Spit jostled against him.

'Well, shift it!'

Behind him, Alex could almost feel the suffocating darkness closing in. But ahead of them, the gang could finally see the source of the draught – a window set high in the wall. Moonlight spilled in through the broken glass like milk.

House pointed.

'Look – I was right. There is a way out!'

Before Inchy had a chance to reply, House leapt into the air and grabbed the ledge, swinging the window open and squeezing through. It

would be a tight fit, but he reckoned he could
. . . he could . . .

'Why have you stopped?' squeaked Inchy.

'It's the window,' said House. 'It's too small.'

'But this is the only way out! You brought us here, and now either we get out or something terrible happens.'

As if in reply, a hoarse, rasping laugh echoed through the cellar.

'I am coming for you!'

Puffing, Alex reached the window only to find Inchy, Spit and Cherry milling around underneath it.

'What's going on?'

'House is stuck.'

'*Stuck?!*'

'Yep,' repeated Inchy. 'Any last requests?'

Dante's pursuing footsteps were closer now. Any moment, he would catch sight of them, and that would be the end.

'House, mate,' said Alex. 'Listen to me. We've got to get through this window.'

'I know,' came the muffled reply. 'But I'm really, really stuck.'

Alex glanced over his shoulder again, and his heart skipped a beat.

In the distance, a shadow, huge and oily, was moving through the darkness towards them. And in the centre of that shadow, glowing like Hell's own fire, were two burning eyes.

Alex cracked.

'House, you big idiot! Get your enormous bulk out of the way or we're all dead, get it?'

'I'm trying! I can't move!'

'You're just giving up!' yelled Alex. 'What are you, a loser? Someone who just sacks it when the going gets tough? Some Guardian Angel you'll be!'

'What did you say?'

Alex took a deep lungful of breath.

'I said there's no way the Guardian Angels will ever take you on. You're just a clumsy, useless wimp!'

It was the longest silence of Alex's life. Then, slowly, House's enormous muscles began to twitch, straining harder than ever before. Suddenly, with a sound of splintering wood, the window frame exploded and House pitched forward and out into the cool night air.

'Go!' screamed Alex.

The gang didn't need telling twice. Scrambling

up the wall, they threw themselves through the window. Picking themselves up off the gravelly playground, all five angels sprinted away, faster than they'd ever run, and they didn't stop until they were back home.

'I don't know whether to laugh or cry,' said Cherry, wiping sweat from her eyes.

'You laugh, I'll cry,' said Inchy, slumping down on to the front doorstep.

'Are you sure he didn't follow us?' asked Spit, with a nervous glance over his shoulder.

'Don't think so,' puffed Cherry. 'He'd never've fitted through that window.'

Alex cautiously approached House.

'I'm sorry for what I said back there.'

House stared back, his face impassive. Alex was suddenly acutely aware of just how much bigger than him House was.

'Erm, I didn't mean it, House, really . . . It was just . . . Well . . .' Alex's voice faded away.

'You gave me the kick I needed,' said House eventually. 'You were right, I was giving up.'

'But the way I said it,' muttered Alex. 'That wasn't right. I'm sorry.'

For a moment, House continued to stare

impassively back. Then his face slowly cracked into a grin.

'Next time we're running away from a demon, you can go in front!'

Alex was just about to agree when, to his horror, the front door opened. Framed in the doorway stood Tabbris, military-neat in matching tartan dressing gown and slippers.

'What time do you call this?'

Something was bothering Alex. He tried to work out what it was during the long lecture on obedience and proper behaviour that Tabbris gave them, but he couldn't quite put his finger on it. In fact, it wasn't until the whole gang were in their beds, Tabbris's telling-off still ringing in their ears, that he realized what it was: back in the cellar, Dante had said that he *knew* someone was there.

How? Dante hadn't seen any of them, and he had said it *before* House's clumsiness had given the gang away. So how could he possibly have known that someone was in the cellar? The team hadn't told anyone what they were planning. It had been a secret shared only among themselves. And it was too much of a coincidence that Dante just happened to be in the right place at the right time.

The answer hit him like a runaway truck. If only the gang knew the plan, then someone from the gang must have told Dante.

Alex felt sick. It was a terrifying thought. Someone had given them away. But who? They were a team – The Wingers. They'd played and studied together for years: the best gang of friends ever to attend Cloud Nine Academy. It just wasn't possible. Big House certainly wouldn't do anything like that; he was too loyal, too much into being a Guardian Angel. Inchy? No, that was idiotic as well. Inchy had a thirst for knowledge, but that didn't mean he'd turn to the Other Side to learn things – he was too sensible for that. And as for Cherry . . . That thought almost made Alex chuckle. A Cherub in cahoots with a demon? Not a chance!

No, there was only one person it could be. He didn't want to believe it, but it was the only answer left. It had to be the person who was always disagreeing with Alex's brilliant plans. The person who'd been so keen to go and research demons, even though he normally hated doing any extra work. The person who'd played so badly in their first footie match that it *must* have been on purpose. The person who'd actually said that life was *better* for people like Dante.

Alex closed his eyes. That person was a traitor.

'Spit,' he murmured as he finally slipped into a fitful sleep. 'It has to be Spit . . .'.

13
Turning the Tables

Alex reached out and tapped Spit on the shoulder. It was early morning and the gang were in a maths lesson. The teacher was absorbed in an elaborate equation scrawled on the board at the front of the classroom. Most of the pupils behind her were having a job staying awake.

Alex tapped again, this time harder.

Spit turned, mouthing a silent 'What?'

Alex didn't say a word. Instead, he quickly handed over a small piece of paper.

Spit opened the note, which just said *Cloakroom. Breaktime. V. important.*

Nodding at Alex, he screwed it up and shoved it into his pocket.

Alex grimaced. He hoped he was wrong, but he'd soon know. This plan was foolproof.

'What's this about, then?' asked Spit. 'No, let me guess; you've discovered that Dante's not a demon at all. He's actually Satan himself and he's here to take over the world and turn it into an enormous pit of fire. Close?'

Spit and Alex were standing alone in a dark corner of the cloakroom where no one would be able to overhear their conversation. Only the usual rattle of the heating pipes above their heads broke the silence.

'Close? Not even warm. But it does involve Dante.'

'Then I'm not interested,' said Spit. 'And I'm not interested because whatever you're about to suggest is going to end up getting us into even more trouble.'

'It won't, trust me,' said Alex.

'Every time you say "trust me" things go bad.'

'Not this time.'

'Every time.'

Spit turned to go, but before he'd taken more than a couple of steps, Alex muttered a few words under his breath.

'What did you say?' asked Spit, turning back.

'I said, "Are you chicken?"'

'It's not about being chicken; it's about not getting into trouble.'

Alex sneered.

'So you *are* chicken, then? Nothing more than a scaredy-cat. Some angel you'll be; nervous of doing anything that might be a little risky.'

'This has nothing to do with being an angel.'

'It's got everything to do with it,' said Alex. 'Tabbris has told us that he's always reporting back to Gabriel. What do you reckon *he'll* think if he finds out that you backed off at the first sign of trouble? Before you know it, you'll be held back a year. Gabriel will have you retaking exams for eternity!'

'He couldn't do that,' said Spit. 'It's not . . .'

His voice trailed off.

'You really want to take that risk?'

Spit paused.

'OK. What have you got to say?'

Alex took a deep breath – it was now or never. Time to test Spit's loyalty.

'I'm meeting the others at lunchtime,' said Alex. 'I've got this awesome idea for a secret weapon to use against Dante. We're meeting at lunch to make it.'

'What, the whole gang?'

'Yup.' Alex looked Spit directly in the eyes. 'You in?'

Spit looked torn for a moment, chewing his bottom lip.

'OK, I'm in.'

'Excellent!' said Alex. 'We're meeting in the old games shed at one o'clock on the dot. We'll sort everything out then, OK? And remember – this is Top Secret. If Dante gets a whiff of it, we're in big trouble.'

The bell rang, bringing breaktime to an end.

'Are you sure it won't get us into trouble anyway?' asked Spit.

'As I said,' smiled Alex, his blue eyes gleaming, 'trust me!'

'That's what I'm worried about.'

At the end of the next lesson, Alex didn't go to lunch. Nor did he tell the others about the meeting with Spit. Instead, he jogged round to the playing fields and hid himself in a bush, his eyes totally focused on the old games shed where Spit should soon be arriving. Now all he had to do was hang around to see who actually turned up. If it was Spit, then Alex's team-mate was in the clear. But if it was someone else – Alex grimaced at the thought – then Spit was the traitor.

At one o'clock precisely, Alex saw a shadow stretch out across the ground in front of the bush as someone approached the old games shed. His heart sank. It was a shadow he recognized, but the figure that cast it wasn't Spit, but someone tall, thin, spindly and angular . . .

Mr Dante crept across the grass and right up to the door of the shed. Then he flung the door open and stalked inside.

'All right, Cloud, what are you up to in here?'

Despite the seriousness of the situation, Alex had to bite his knuckle to stop himself giggling as he listened to Dante rummaging around in the empty shed, muttering curses. Eventually, the geography teacher emerged, dusty and furious, and stormed off in the direction of the school.

As Dante disappeared, though, so did Alex's

excitement. His plan had worked like magic, but success felt about as hollow as the growing emptiness in his stomach. Confirming his suspicions about Spit had been simple enough. Now came the hard part – working out how to tell the others.

'So,' said House, finally seeming to understand what Alex had spent the last ten minutes trying to explain, 'you told Spit to meet us in the shed . . .'

Alex nodded.

'. . . and instead of going to the meeting, you just watched from a bush to see if someone other than Spit would turn up.'

'Absolutely,' said Alex. 'And someone else did turn up – Dante. But he couldn't possibly have known about the meeting. Just like he couldn't have known we were in the cellar last night. Unless Spit told him.'

There was a pause. The gang listened to the sound of running water from the bathroom next door where Spit was having a shower.

House frowned.

'Did you ask him why he wasn't there at one o'clock?'

'Of course,' replied Alex. 'He *claims* Dante gave him a lunchtime detention for running in the corridors. But I don't believe it.'

Inchy didn't look convinced. 'I just can't believe Spit's a traitor.'

'Yeah, why would he turn against us?' asked Cherry. 'Maybe Dante goes to the games shed every day, you know, as part of his job or something.'

'Bit of a coincidence that he turns up at *just* the time I'd told Spit to meet me there, don't you think?' said Alex.

'But Spit's one of us,' said Inchy. 'I know he's sarcastic, but he's no way a Hell's Angel!'

'Perhaps he wants to be,' suggested Cherry.

'No one wants to be a Hell's Angel,' said House.

'Well,' sighed Alex, 'one thing's for sure: the only people who knew about the meeting in the old games shed were me and Spit. Seeing as Dante turned up to find us, I'm guessing Spit told him it was happening; it's the only answer.' He paused. 'We just have to accept it – Spit's a traitor.'

'So now what do we do?' asked Cherry. 'We're a man down! It's not looking good, is it?'

'And if Spit *is* a traitor,' said Inchy, 'then there's

a good chance Dante knows exactly what we're up to, what we've been doing and what we've found out.'

'We've got no choice,' said Alex. 'We have to act now, or everything we've found out has been for nothing.'

Alex's face turned very serious as he looked at his friends.

'We need to get the egg out of the cellar before Dante moves it.'

Alex held up a hand to forestall Inchy's objections. 'We can figure out what we're going to do with it later. Maybe we can use it to blackmail Dante or something. But tonight we go to the cellar and steal the egg. Without Spit.'

Alex lay staring into the darkness, waiting for the signal. He dug his nails into the palms of his hands — he had to stay awake. That was vital. Then, just as he felt himself drifting off, something soft and smelly thumped into his face. A second later, Inchy appeared at his side.

'Spit's asleep.'

'And you needed to throw a sock at me to tell me that?'

'It was all I had to hand,' whispered Inchy. 'But

he's definitely asleep; his breathing's changed and he's not moving at all.'

'You absolutely sure?' asked Alex.

Inchy nodded.

'Then let's go,' said Alex.

'Are you certain this is a good idea? Tabbris really flipped out last time he caught us up after eight o'clock. We're supposed to be grounded. If he catches us again . . .'

'We've been through this,' growled Alex. 'There's no other choice. Now let's get going.'

Inchy slunk back off into the dark.

'House?' hissed Alex.

'Ready,' whispered House, and a shadow dropped silently from the top bunk to land in front of Alex.

'That was impressive. You didn't knock anything over.'

'Practice makes perfect.'

As the gang tiptoed past Spit's bed, they made extra sure that they didn't make a sound. With a last look at Spit, his snoring body shrouded in a heavy duvet, Alex slipped out into the corridor and closed the door softly behind him.

In the darkness of the bedroom, Spit's eyes opened.

14
Demon's Lair

'Is it me, or is it even hotter than last night?'

Inchy was standing behind Alex and Big House, a torch in his shaking hands. Cherry was next to him, an arrow strung in her bow. It was dark and warm, like the inside of a sleeping bag, and ahead of them in the silent shadows lay the door to the cellar.

It had been surprisingly simple to get away from the house. Tabbris had been fast asleep in front of the fire, his medals spread out on his lap, when the gang snuck past. Now they just had to worry about getting back in. Assuming they came back at all.

'Think that'll be useful?' asked House, nodding at Cherry's bow.

'No idea,' shrugged Cherry nervously. 'I've never tried firing Cherub arrows at demons before.'

She tried to laugh, but the sound caught in her throat and turned into a stifled squeak.

'I'm not sure about this,' muttered Inchy. 'Doesn't feel right.'

'Did you ask those Justice Scales of yours, Inch?'

Inchy nodded at Cherry.

'Yeah, and they just sort of . . . hung in the balance.'

'What does that mean?'

'Simple,' said Inchy. 'Either this could all go very, very well, we win and end up as heroes . . .'

Inchy's voice trailed off.

'Or?' prompted Cherry.

'Or everything goes very, very badly, we lose and end up being smashed into tiny pieces by the hugely powerful and very evil Mr Dante.'

'Ah.'

'We'll be fine,' said Alex. 'So long as we stick together.'

Behind his back, Inchy and Cherry exchanged glances. They were both thinking the same thing. It was too late for sticking together – the team was already broken. Spit had been left behind.

Alex reached out, turned the handle of the cellar door and pushed.

'After you.'

House grimaced.

'Do you really want me to go first? After what happened last time?'

'Good point. Well, after me, I suppose.'

Alex took a tentative step on to the stairs.

'I can't see a thing,' whispered Cherry.

'Well, don't trip up and fall into me,' came Inchy's nervous voice from the blackness.

'I'm not House.'

'In this darkness, everyone's House.'

'I think we're at the bottom of the steps,' said Alex quietly.

'Let's rock 'n' roll, ladies and gents,' said House, cracking his knuckles.

Inchy looked at House, shaking his head.

'Do they teach you these terrible lines when you become a Guardian Angel, or do you just make them up yourself?'

Before House could reply, Cherry muttered, 'Something's not right. It feels different tonight. It's like something's missing.'

'Spit?'

Cherry shook her head.

'No, that's not it, although it does feel weird to be doing this without him.'

House spoke up. 'It's getting hotter and hotter, so let's just grab the egg and get out.'

'That's it!' exclaimed Cherry.

'What's it?'

'It's hotter!'

'What's that got to do with it?' asked Alex. 'We're wasting valuable time.'

'It's even hotter than last night, but the pipes aren't rattling!'

House, Alex and Inchy listened; the deafening silence rang in their ears.

'She's right,' said Inchy. 'Why do you think that is?'

Alex shrugged.

'The pipes only rattle when the heating is on. So it must've been turned off.'

'Then why is it even hotter than before?' asked Cherry.

'How should I know?' said Alex. 'Do I look like a plumber? All I want to do is to grab the egg and get out of here. The longer we stand around discussing the ins and outs of the school heating system, the more chance we've got of being discovered.'

'I'm just saying –'

'It doesn't matter what you're just saying. Let's finish what we came here to do, OK?'

'Fine,' huffed Cherry. 'But don't say I didn't warn you.'

The gang crept on through the eerie silence, towards the red glow that marked the room where the furnace lay. After what seemed like hours, they arrived. Peering through the doorway, the angels could see no sign of Dante. But the furnace was hotter than ever, almost white hot, and the demon egg was still sitting on top of it.

'Right,' said Alex, his tone hushed. 'Here goes.' He handed House a small rucksack. 'Be careful.'

House looked confused.

'Why've you given me this?'

'To collect the egg,' replied Alex.

'You have to be joking,' said House, backing off. 'You're asking the clumsiest person here to go and collect a very important and dangerous egg? Are you nuts? And you know I'm even worse when I'm nervous!'

'He's got a point,' said Inchy, then turned to House. 'No offence.'

'I'll do it,' said Cherry, stepping forward and grabbing the bag. 'Then we leave, OK?'

'Fine by me,' replied Alex.

Alex, Inchy and House stared in silence as Cherry scampered forward, using her arm to shield her face from the intense heat of the furnace. Without pausing, she scooped up the glowing green egg, slipped it into the rucksack and dashed back to the gang.

'Sorted,' she said proudly.

Then it happened.

With a sound like rats scuttling inside a hollow wall, a creeping wave of shadow flowed out from behind the numerous pipes that led from the furnace, buffeting the gang with a wave of intense dry heat. It spread like ink on wet paper, surrounding them, even obscuring the glow of the furnace and pulling the air from their lungs in gasps. The shadow oozed closer until, within its darkness, tiny eyes appeared. Eyes set deep into horrible, pointy faces laced with sneers and snarls.

Closer still it came, and soon the gang saw that the vile faces, with their eyes beady and yellow, were connected to spindly little bodies – no more than skin stretched over bent twisted skeletons. The heat generated by these tiny bodies grew stronger as the creatures drew ever closer to the young angels. The air crackled with a mix of rattling laughter and sharp cackles, punctuated by the sound of small feet scratching on the stone floor.

'Imps!' squealed Inchy. 'I hate imps!'

'Don't be such a baby,' snapped Cherry. 'House can handle a few imps.'

'Yeah,' said House, taking a tentative step towards the tiny creatures. 'There are quite a lot of them, though.'

Then another sound, like a tattered old newspaper being torn by a harsh breeze, cut through the noise the imps were making. Their many shadows backed away, to be replaced by a single shadow even more terrible. It stretched across the gang: long arms ending in sharp-clawed hands; bent, muscular legs; a scarred torso and wings so huge they seemed to enfold the whole world.

Finally, the shadow spoke. The gang all recognized the voice at once, but it did not come from the face of a teacher. Instead, it gushed forth from the fanged mouth of a demon.

'Hello, Cloud.'

And the laughter of Mr Dante reverberated through the cellars like thunder.

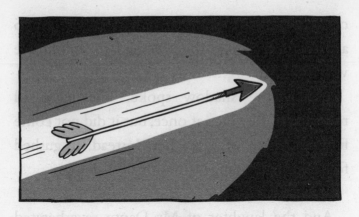

15
Face Off

'You know, I always wanted a pet angel,' said Dante, his wings scraping the walls, sending chunks of rubble skittering across the floor. 'But to have four? Why, what a treat that will be!'

The gang were trapped: Dante in front of them, a horde of vile, stinking imps crowding all around.

'We're not pets,' said Cherry, sounding far more defiant than she felt.

'You will be, my dear,' said Dante, leaning forward, an evil grin slicing his face. 'And you will learn to do my every command, to obey my every whim, no matter how awful it may sound. Allow me to *demon*strate.'

The gang watched as Dante turned to the imps and pointed.

'You!'

A pathetic imp edged forward, one foot dragging behind the other. It stood alone, cowering between Dante and the gang.

'Fetch me coal from the furnace,' said Dante.

The imp didn't even hesitate. It turned, ran to the furnace, thrust its hand through the grate and returned with a red-hot coal clutched in its smoking fingers.

'More,' said Dante, not even looking at what the imp had brought.

The imp dropped the coal, ran back to the furnace, and this time returned with both hands piled high with scorching embers.

'You see?' said Dante as flames started to lick around the imp's hands. 'I command and they obey. You'll soon get used to the arrangement, I'm sure. Now, if you don't mind . . .'

Dante opened a huge claw expectantly.

'Are you just going to leave the poor thing like that?' asked Cherry, looking at the imp. Flames had now almost fully engulfed it.

Dante smiled.

'Of course not,' he said, and he reached out, plucked the imp from the ground and popped it into his mouth, coals and all.

The sound of crunching made Alex's stomach churn.

'I'm not going to be eaten by a demon,' muttered House. 'No way. That's *so* not happening to me.'

'Come,' said Dante, opening his hand once more. 'If you give me the egg now, I promise that your pain will be more, well, bearable.'

Alex knew he had to think. If ever he could do with a genius plan it was now. It was his fault that his friends were in this mess. He just needed more time to come up with something.

He faced Dante, wide-eyed.

'How did you turn Spit?'

House, Cherry and Inchy all turned to look at Alex.

'What are you doing?' muttered Inchy, under his breath. Alex ignored him.

'Come on. How did you do it? What did you offer him? It must have been quite something to turn an angel to follow your stinking ideas.'

'Alex!' hissed Cherry. 'Don't wind him up!'

'What are you wittering on about now, Cloud?' snarled Dante. 'Every time you open your mouth, I'm tempted to tear out your tongue and wear it round my neck.'

'Spit,' said Alex, trying to ignore the rather horrible threat. 'You turned him traitor. What did you offer him that was enough to turn him against us, his friends? Just how much were we worth?'

Dante laughed.

'And why do you think I would bother to "turn" even one of you, when I can quite easily swat you all like flies?'

'You knew we were here last night,' said Alex, still frantically trying to think of a way out of this desperate situation. 'And you knew about the meeting at the old games shed. The only people who knew about that were me and Spit.'

He looked Dante right in the eyes, hoping that his voice wasn't shaking too much. 'I made it up – there was no meeting! But you still came, didn't you? Spit told you about it. He betrayed us.'

Just saying the words made Alex feel so angry that it was all he could do to stop himself screaming.

'Cloud,' said Dante, 'I have no need to recruit spies from the student body; I have my own army of them right here. And, as you have seen, they are utterly loyal, even to the point of death.'

Dante gestured at the dozens of cackling imps that surrounded them.

'But how did *they* find out about it?' asked Alex.

'Look,' said Dante, gesturing expansively around the cellar. 'What do you see?'

'Pipes,' said Alex. 'But what've pipes got to do with it?'

Dante let his head fall back in a terrible laugh.

'Of course!' cried Inchy. 'The imps have been running around in the pipes. That's why they've been rattling so much – and why the school's been so hot. The imps must have overheard you talking to Spit about the meeting!'

'Clever boy,' said Dante, now turning to look at Inchy. 'You'll make a very useful pet. Yes, my imps have done a wonderful job of keeping the egg warm for me – with the added bonus of keeping me informed as to the goings-on in this silly little school.'

Alex felt his breath catch in his throat. He wanted to be sick, to run away, to hide. How could he have been so wrong?

His whole body shaking, Alex stared at Dante.

'It wasn't Spit,' he said faintly. 'It was the imps. They told you everything. It wasn't Spit.'

'Indeed, Mr Cloud,' sneered Dante. 'How little faith you put in your so-called friends. But enough of this; hand me the egg at once!'

Dante stretched out his taloned hand towards the gang.

Everyone looked at Alex, but he seemed dumbstruck.

Cherry spoke up instead. 'If we run, there's no way you can catch all of us,' she shouted. 'One of us will escape. And we'll call down Special Operations, and that'll be it – you're history!'

Once again Dante laughed, as if the whole evening was one enormous joke.

'Special Operations?' he scoffed. 'Do you really think that those blundering fools concern me? Besides, I have allies of my own in this pathetic town.'

Dante growled, his wings flapped, and the walls of the cellar seemed to shake, dust and rock falling around them. He stared at the gang, his hideous face low, his eyes glowing like fire in the darkness.

'Let your Special Operations come!' he said, his voice an avalanche of rocks and cracking ice. 'My master will destroy you all!'

'What's he going on about?' whispered House, but Alex wasn't listening, couldn't hear. All he could think about was Spit and how he'd misjudged everything so spectacularly. If only he'd realized. If only he'd thought things through. But it was too late now. Too late to do anything.

Dante was standing tall now, hands stretched high.

'And my master,' continued Dante, 'will bring the kingdom of Hell on Earth! And you will all kneel before us!'

Realization flashed across Inchy's face.

'I knew I'd seen someone else!' he said. 'Remember? When I first followed him into the cellar.'

'So who *is* this master?' asked Cherry. 'What's he on about?'

But there was no time for anyone to answer, as Dante shot out a long-fingered hand and plucked the zombie-like Alex from the ground.

'Now, give me back that egg before I crush Cloud – one bone at a time!'

Alex looked down at his gang. They were his friends, the people who had trusted him.

And now everything was finished because of him. Everything.

And it was at that moment that a plan popped into his head.

There was no time to think about it. Alex just had to hope he knew his remaining friends better than he'd known Spit.

'OK, you win. House, give him the egg – and be careful.'

House looked up.

'Are you serious?'

'Yes,' said Alex. 'Just be very, *very* careful, OK?'

House shuffled his feet awkwardly. Alex could already see the nervous sweat beading on his brow.

'Umm.'

'I'll do it,' said Cherry, pulling open the rucksack.

'No!' growled Alex, through gritted teeth. 'Not you; House. Let him do it.'

For a moment, the gang just stared at him,

confused. Then, suddenly, the penny dropped. Cherry and Inchy understood.

'Go on, House,' said Cherry, holding the open bag out towards the big angel.

'Yeah,' added Inchy. 'Just be really *careful*.'

His hands shaking, House plucked the egg out of the bag, holding it as if it was a bomb. It barely fitted into his cupped hands, glowing green in the gloomy cellar.

House looked up at Dante and started to walk slowly towards him. He didn't really understand what was going on, but Alex had given him a job to do. Alex always trusted him, even if he did get nervous sometimes. And House wasn't about to let down his best mate. It wasn't too difficult, really. Alex had told him what to do: just carry the egg to Dante and be very, *very* careful. The last thing he wanted to do in this situation was to —

House tripped.

The egg spun high into the air.

With a roar, Dante dropped Alex to the floor with a thump, grabbed wildly at the egg – and missed.

Almost in slow motion, the gang watched as the egg turned over and over in the air before smashing into the ground and exploding in a huge burst of fire and acid.

Dante screamed. His wings went into overdrive – flailing around, smashing into the walls and bringing down lumps of rock from the roof. He turned, his teeth bared and wet with drool, dribbling to the floor.

'I will eat your souls!' he screeched.

The gang cowered, waiting for the inevitable.

The last thing any of them expected was a large yellow balloon to smack Dante right in the face and explode in a shower of water. It was very quickly followed by three more. Each balloon was a different colour, but they all burst on impact, spraying water all over the furious demon and his imps.

The gang turned to see where the balloons had been launched from.

'Spit!' yelled Alex.

Sure enough, standing in the doorway, a long orange balloon balanced on his left foot, was Spit. His hair was hanging loose across his face, and his eyes, narrow and keen, were utterly focused on Dante.

With a flick of his leg, Spit sent the orange

balloon flying across the cave, as if it were an oversized football. His aim was as true as a perfect corner kick, but Dante was ready this time and caught the balloon in one hand, bursting it.

Dante's laugh slammed through the cave, his huge chest steaming as the liquid evaporated away. He stared down at Spit.

'You pitiful, childish fool! Did you really think that a Fire Demon could be harmed by water!'

Spit eyeballed Dante, brushing the hair from his eyes.

'You're right,' he said. 'Only an idiot would throw water at a demon.'

Dante's face was torn by a snarl.

'But I'm not an idiot, and guess what?'

Spit grinned.

'That isn't just water.'

Something certainly wasn't right. The cloud of steam rising from Dante's body wasn't slowing. In fact, it seemed to be growing thicker, more like smoke. And at his feet, the imps were exploding like popcorn, vanishing in little puffs of black.

'What have you done?' roared the demon.

'It's silver, dung-breath,' said Spit brightly. 'Water mixed with lots and lots of silver.'

'Look!' yelled Inchy. 'His face! It's crumbling!'

'He's turning to stone!' shouted Alex. 'Outstanding!'

It was true. The skin of Dante's face was cracking and peeling, like an old scab. As the gang watched, one of his wings suddenly snapped off, falling to the ground, where it exploded in a shower of gritty black dust.

Then his other wing crumbled. A hand followed – then the rest of the arm. Dante roared again, shaking the cave.

But he was finding it harder to move. His body was seizing up. With a final shriek, Dante fell silent and still, his huge demonic form frozen where it stood, like a gigantic statue.

Alex looked at Cherry.

'I'm thinking now's as good a time as any to test out your new archery skills.'

Without a word, Cherry raised her bow, took aim, let fly an arrow.

And Dante exploded into a cloud of rubble and dust.

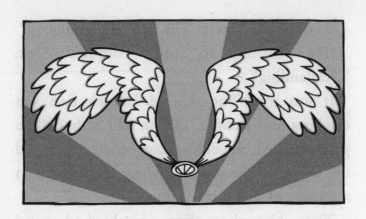

16
High School Heroes

'Did you honestly think I was asleep?'

It was the next day, and Spit was standing between Alex and Cherry just outside the old shed in the woods at the bottom of the garden. In front of them, under Inchy's direction, House was digging a large hole.

'What else were we supposed to think?' replied Alex. 'Your eyes were shut and you were snoring.'

'And you actually thought I was on Dante's side?'

Alex paused, opened his mouth and then shut

it again, in a very good impression of a goldfish.

Spit shook his head.

'What is it with you? Just because I don't love getting into trouble all the time, you think that automatically makes me the bad guy? One of us has to keep our feet on the ground – wings or no wings.'

Cherry glanced at the two boys and then walked over to the hole to give a few needless instructions to House. This was between Alex and Spit.

'Look, I'm sorry,' said Alex, his shoulders slumped. 'But what was I supposed to think? I mean, it's not like you were really into fighting Dante, was it?'

'How odd – not to want to fight a Level Four Demon,' snapped Spit. 'But that doesn't mean I'd betray you!'

Spit raised his voice.

'And then you tried to trick me! I mean, what's all that about?'

'I don't know,' said Alex.

'Yes, you do. You're always scheming, always complicating things with your stupid plans.'

They fell silent.

'Look,' said Alex eventually, 'I just want to say . . . What you did back in the cellar. That was . . . Well, it was really cool.'

Spit looked up.

'I mean it,' said Alex, brightening. 'It was awesome! Those waterbombs were just the best thing ever! They totally destroyed Dante! And your silky skills are back up to their normal standards. You may have played like a muppet in the game against The Black Crows, but you were brilliant when you needed to be. You're a demon slayer!'

At this, the rest of the gang turned back to Spit.

'It was pretty fantastic,' said Cherry.

'Work of genius,' said Inchy.

'And it made more mess than I've *ever* made,' smiled House, shoulder-deep in the hole, his face streaked with sweat and mud.

'But where did you find enough silver?' asked Alex. 'I mean, you must have needed loads. Where did you get it?'

A faint proud smile crept across Spit's face.

'Never you mind. But it was a good job I did, wasn't it?'

'And how did you know we were in trouble?' asked Cherry.

'Well, for a start, it was Alex's plan, which is never a good thing.'

Alex almost smiled.

'And I figured that without you lot cramping my style I might be able to do something. So I dug the waterbombs out of the Lucky Dip and followed you down into the cellar. From then on I just sort of, er, *winged* it.'

Everyone laughed.

'Thanks,' said Alex. 'And I'm sorry. I mean it. Truce?'

Spit took Alex's outstretched hand.

'Truce.' Spit grinned. 'After all, every gang of angels needs a demon slayer!'

'And you're never going to let us forget that, are you?'

Amid the laughter, it was House who asked the question that they'd all been pondering.

'So when do we get our heroes' welcome back into Heaven, then?'

'Ah,' said Alex. 'That might be a bit tricky. I mean, Dante's been destroyed and the egg's been smashed, so there's no proof that there ever was a demon in Green Hill.'

'What about all the stuff in the secret room behind Dante's cupboard?' asked Cherry.

'Gone,' replied Alex. 'When House and I went back this morning to check it out, the room was empty.'

Inchy sucked in a deep breath.

'Dante did say he had allies in the town. Maybe they came and took everything during the night.'

'Well, not quite everything.'

Everyone turned to see what was lying in Alex's hands.

'*The Book of the Dead*,' said Cherry, her voice quiet.

'We could show that to Tabbris,' suggested House.

'But it doesn't prove that we destroyed a demon,' said Inchy sadly. 'We could have found the book in the library for all he knows. Even if Tabbris believed us, which I very much doubt, we'd have to tell him about sneaking out of the house again, and going up against Dante without telling him. I don't think he'd be very pleased.'

'So, no heroes' welcome?'

'No, House, not this time,' replied Alex.

'No parade?'

'Nope.'

'No —'

'No nothing,' snapped Spit.

'What do we do with the book, then?' Cherry raised her eyebrows at the others.

Alex turned to House.

'That hole ready?'

'As ready as a hole can be,' said House, climbing out.

Alex turned to Spit, handing him the book.

'Here,' he said. 'You throw it in. Finish off Dante good and proper.'

Spit took the book and held it for a moment.

'The *Necronomicon*. It could be very useful –'

'Spit!'

'Just kidding.'

And he tossed it into the hole.

'What good is burying it going to do anyway?' asked Cherry, as House started piling earth on top of the book.

'It's the best we can do,' said Inchy. 'We can't destroy it; so unless you fancy some pretty scary bedtime reading?'

'OK, burying it is fine by me,' said Cherry hurriedly. 'But what about the "master" that Dante was talking about? Won't he be looking for it? That could be really dodgy.'

'It *is* really dodgy,' said Inchy as the hole slowly filled up. 'Because it means that there's probably another demon in Green Hill. One even more powerful than Dante.'

'That sounds bad,' muttered House.

'It is,' grinned Spit. 'Lucky you've got a demon slayer in the gang, isn't it?'

'You're not so ugly when you smile,' said Alex.

'And you're not so annoying when you shut up,' Spit shot back.

Before Alex could reply, a terrible cry rent the air.

'Dante!' moaned House. 'He's back!'

'Doesn't sound like Dante,' replied Alex, as the cry came again. 'More like Tabbris.'

'He doesn't sound happy.'

'He probably isn't,' said Spit.

Alex turned.

'Why not?'

Spit shrugged shiftily, and suddenly a terrible thought occurred to Alex.

'That silver dust in the waterbombs. Where did you get it?'

'You know. Around.'

'Spit. Where did you get it?'

'Oh,' said Spit, sidling towards the trees. 'I just smashed Tabbris's Order of Raphael medal into tiny little bits.'

For a moment the rest of the gang stood dumbstruck. Then they heard Tabbris coming down the garden.

'Vandals! Thieves! Wait until Gabriel hears about this!'

Alex glanced at his friends. They may have defeated Dante and uncovered a demonic plot in Green Hill, but if they still needed Tabbris to approve their return, it didn't look like they'd be going back to Heaven any time soon.

'Don't panic – I have a plan.'

The team stared at Alex.

'Run!'

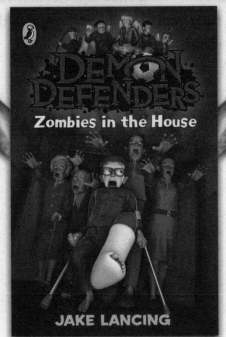

Introducing Diary of a Wimpy Kid!

Let me get something straight – this is a journal, not a diary. I'm not going to write about my feelings or anything. The only reason I agreed to do this is because it'll come in handy one day when I'm rich and famous . . .

MORONS

But for now I'm stuck in middle school with a bunch of morons.

Today is the first day of school and I, Greg Heffley, am taking you with me.

Just don't expect me to be all 'Dear Diary' this and 'Dear Diary' that.

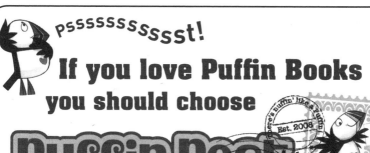

It all started with a Scarecrow

Puffin is well over sixty years old.
Sounds ancient, doesn't it? But Puffin has never been
so lively. We're always on the lookout for the next big
idea, which is how it began all those years ago.

Penguin Books was a big idea from the mind of
a man called Allen Lane, who in 1935 invented
the quality paperback and changed the world.
**And from great Penguins, great Puffins grew,
changing the face of children's books forever.**

The first four Puffin Picture Books were hatched in 1940 and the
first Puffin story book featured a man with broomstick arms called
Worzel Gummidge. In 1967 Kaye Webb, Puffin Editor, started the
Puffin Club, promising to **'make children into readers'**.
She kept that promise and over 200,000 children became
devoted Puffineers through their quarterly installments of
Puffin Post, which is now back for a new generation.

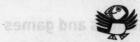

Many years from now, we hope you'll look back and
remember Puffin with a smile. **No matter what your age
or what you're into, there's a Puffin for everyone.**
The possibilities are endless, but one thing is for sure:
whether it's a picture book or a paperback, a sticker book
or a hardback, **if it's got that little Puffin
on it – it's bound to be good.**